We Found It Ranch

We Found It Ranch

Jack Bernard Rhodes

ISBN: Hardcover   978-1-7960-3169-0
            Softcover   978-1-7960-3168-3
            eBook   978-1-7960-3167-6

Print information available on the last page.

Rev. date: 05/02/2019

To order additional copies of this book, contact:
Xlibris
1-888-795-4274
www.Xlibris.com
Orders@Xlibris.com
795642

CHAPTER ONE

MY DAD LONGED to get back to his roots. He was burned out and sick of his sales management job that he held since 1950, the year my parents were married. He was sick of the constant travel all over Tennessee, conducting sales meetings and listening to the route salesmen make excuses for their lack of sales productivity. He was fed up with the greasy restaurant food and lumpy hotel beds and depressed over the isolation. It had been fifteen years and he was ready for a change. He fantasized about having a home-every-night job and buying a farm to tend to, in his spare time.

He dreamed to one day get out of our cramped bungalow-style home located on a noisy street with yapping dogs, lawn machinery, loud music, teenagers acting like teenagers, and no privacy. The noise pollution from constant passing traffic of a nearby major highway was nerve-racking. He felt hemmed in with the homes positioned too close together with narrowly spaced yards and everyone knew everyone else's business. He felt smothered and he wanted out. He wanted to escape. He knew if he diligently searched, he could find a more satisfying, family-oriented career. He fantasized about buying a farm. Others have done it and why not him? They're on the market, at reasonable prices, and he was determined get his to the point of obsession. "The time is now, while the market is soft," he would tell my mom. "On summer nights, we can hear the beautiful sound of insects. Nothing like what we hear in the city. Early in the morning we will hear all of the species of birds singing at the same time. We can actually grow our own vegetables! Imagine that. Homegrown is ten times better than the crap we buy at the grocery store. A farm will give us a more quality life. We deserve it."

Mom despised the idea of taking on the burden and debt of a farm. The thought of a hardscrabble life of a farmer's wife left her petrified. It was just plain crazy and scary too. She thought such an existence to be unaffordable, dreadfully lonely, and too many spiders and snakes. Her phobia was snakes ever since she was a child, when she swore that a snake was chasing her. Besides, she was happy living within the city limits. Everything was close. A farm would mean long drives to get to any place where conveniences are necessary for a happy and sane lifestyle. She wanted to be near the shops where she could drive to quickly and leisurely browse all day, as she sometimes would do. She didn't care to be burdened with a long drive home. She couldn't imagine not being near the grocery stores. She needed to be where she has always had the practicality of dashing out to get a missing ingredient for a recipe or pick up milk or eggs. Her best friend, Roxane, had been styling her hair for the last ten years. If she lived on a farm and if it was too far away, then she would have to get her hair fixed elsewhere, but where? Where could she find a salon in the country, by someone that could do a decent job? She missed Dad when he was away, but it was the kind of life she'd grown accustomed to. Ever since her marriage, she had felt a sense of security that she was unwilling to give up. The kind of change that Dad wanted worried her. Her hands were full, already, as a housewife and a mother for my older sister, Nancy, and me. She didn't want to be troubled with farm life.

Nancy wasn't fond of the thought of moving, naturally because of leaving her friends and school, but she had been aware of the talk of moving since she was small. She became oblivious of the idea over time. She was in her own world in 1965, and she embraced the adolescent fashion craze for that era. She was obsessed with her 45's of The Stones, The Kinks, and the Beatles. Her bedroom walls were littered with posters of the top rock-and-roll singers and even one of Mick Jagger's image that seemed to look down at her while she lay in bed. She had *Tiger Beat* pullouts of Paul McCartney and Lulu. Her window was draped with a groovy beaded, curtain valance, and a cool fringed lighting hanging from her ceiling. She was the cool kid in school, who flaunted her flipped bob in front of other girls who adulated her. She was also the class president, who earned perfect grades. She would string along sex-crazed boys and teased them mercilessly. She would be a sophomore next year, and she looked forward to the best that was yet to come.

They are at it again. It seemed regularly during my preteen childhood years that my parents argued over my dad's yearning to buy a farm. "Give up this ridiculous dream, Jake!" Mom admonished to Dad, who she'd been married to for fifteen years. "I hate it whenever you get this bull-headed idea in your head about buying a farm! Just stop it, stop it, STOP IT!"

"Now, relax, Lily. It'll be good for the kids. Living on a farm will teach the boy the value of work. Nancy is fourteen. She's a teen now. This will be a healthier environment for her and will keep her away from bad influences of the other kids, in the city."

"Me relax? Would you come to your senses? Levi is only ten and you are behaving more like a child than he is. Nancy is a good girl. She knows right from wrong. For goodness' sake, we live in Nashville, not New York!"

I actually favored the idea of living on a farm. After all, Dad promised to buy me a horse and we would have some chickens for me to care for and feed. There would be lots of space for "Zoomer," our collie, to play too! He said that after we settle in, he would eventually find another occupation that would allow him to be home every night. For me, it was a fantasy. I was at that age where I believed that my dad always did what's best for the family.

"I think I found a farm that's affordable," Dad said cautiously to Mom. "Let's all take a drive this weekend and have a look."

Mom glared discerningly and finally bellowed, "Ohhh, Jake, you can't be serious! We're in debt now. We can't afford it at any price."

"We can afford this one. It's only twelve thousand dollars and it has forty acres. Think of it. It'll pay for itself in no time! It's a farm. There's always money to be made on a farm!"

*　*　*　*　*

"Get up, Levi!" Dad shouted at me excitedly for the third time. It was 6:15 the following Saturday morning, and he was anxious for all of us to get started on the two-hour drive, for the home viewing. I've been anticipating today's trip there too, except for getting up so early. Mom had been mad at Dad ever since he announced that he called a real estate agent to see the farm at 10 am today. My parents had bickered from the night before to early morning. Nancy, who sided with our mom, still doubted that moving away–and to a farm too–would ever happen.

In 1965, before the feminist movement, the father was still the head of the house, in most instances, and it was no different in ours. Therefore, off we went, to a destination that would eventually change our lives to extremes. Dad's determination to keep the morning appointment to view the farm was not swayed, despite Nancy's excuses that that the trip would ruin her Saturday plans. Not even Mom's scornful objections could not deter him. Dad and I talked about what life could be like on a farm, as he drove. We talked about how we would drink fresh milk from our own cow, have eggs from our own chickens and a horse to ride too! Dad and I could not contain our excitement. Mom and my sister just glanced at each other as they sat in stunned silence.

Mom's worry had caused her to rest fitfully the night before, and she nodded off during the drive. "You must have taken a wrong turn. This is a gravel road," Mom expressed in dismay as she was awakened by the sound of pebbles popping underneath the car. "Turn around at that old farmhouse, Jake."

What stood before us was a slightly neglected, small, white frame house, built around the middle of the last century. The stories that it could tell seem like it could be those of difficult farm labor of yesteryear and agonizing loneliness too, considering its location on a gravel road in a scarcely populated rural area. It was miles away from the nearest town of Morris. The barn that stood about a hundred yards behind it was unpainted and leaning slightly.

"The realtor said it would be the second house to the left on Old Eagle Road, so this must be it!" Dad exclaimed.

"What a dump and we're in the middle of nowhere!" Nancy quipped. "Ya'll go on, I'll just sit in the car."

"Forget it, Jake! You brought us out here for this? You have lost your mind! That house isn't fit to live in. I'll stay in the car too. I already know I don't like it," Mom complained.

"We've come this far. You should at least get out of the car and stretch your legs, and take a look," Dad said excitedly.

Just at that moment, Elmer Yager, a portly older man, stepped out of the house, waving, and yelled, "Ya'll must be the new buyers! Don't be shy. Get out and look around. My wife and I have been waiting. Welcome to the 'Circle Y' ranch!"

Just when Mom thought it couldn't get any worse, she eyed a small building behind the house and she shrieked, "That's an outhouse! Jake, this old run-down shack doesn't even have an indoor. I have seen enough!"

"I've seen enough too," Nancy chimed in.

"Relax, both of you," Dad insisted. "We are getting a great deal on this place. We'll build a bathroom and install indoor plumbing too. A mortgage company has already approved extra on the loan for the additions. We are not turning around now, so let's get out and at least look at everything."

Mom screamed. "Damn you, Jake! You didn't say anything about it having no indoor bathroom. This house is not fit to live in, no matter what!" Mom was crying now. "You signed a loan for this dump and kept it from me. Damn you, damn you, DAMN YOU!"

"I haven't done anything yet. We are only looking and I didn't sign a loan. I only applied for one. The owner, Mr. Yager, is on the porch waiting. Let's get out of the car and meet him. Let's not be rude. Get ahold of yourself, Lily."

"This farm has the potential to be the best in the county, and call me Elmer. It's forty acres and five of it is wooded. The rest is pasture for grazing, growing hay and corn. You will have a large barn that has plenty of room for storing. Don't forget that I'm throwing in Sam. There's also a pond that's stocked with plenty of catfish and it's all flat land. Sam is the horse's name, by the way," said Elmer.

He has a horse and it will be ours if Dad buys the farm and there's a pond with fish! "Can I ride the horse?" I asked excitedly.

"Of course, son. We'll go saddle him up. I'm throwing in the saddle too," Elmer added cheerily. In a panic, Mom tried to object, but Elmer assured us that Sam was gentle, easy to ride, and loves children. "My wife, Liz, is preparing our lunch, and almost all the food is from our land. She loves to cook for company. We are both so glad you came, and we want all of you to spend the whole day here. Ya'll are gonna love this farm, so let's go saddle Sam so your boy and all of you can ride and then we'll eat lunch! We have all day to see the farm, and we'll meet some of the neighbors too. Everyone is very friendly and eager to help you get settled!"

This was my very first ride on a horse, and being on it made me a little nervous. Dad slapped it on the rear, and it began to trot. Since I was unprepared, I went tumbling and hit the ground hard. Dad told me to get back on, but I was hesitant so he ordered me back on. He said falling off is the best experience and by getting back on quickly, I would have no time to think about falling off again. I also quickly became a natural horseback rider soon after that, or at least in my own mind. This was the most important horseback lesson I received.

Dad rode Sam too, but Mom and Nancy would not come near the horse or the barn. Liz came out and invited them in, to get acquainted. The first thing Lily noticed was how much larger the house looked on the inside and had at one time been remodeled, but she was puzzled that no indoor plumbing had been added. Mom asked if there was any plumbing inside. Liz said they had installed siding on the walls and put in new floors but ran out of money to do more. Liz claimed they were used to not having any plumbing anyway. "We draw water from the well, behind the house. It's a lot healthier than city water." Liz detected their indignation and seemed to be sympathetic with their objections to country living. "It'll take time for city folks to get used to this way of life but you will get adjusted to it and start to love it before you know it," Liz said reassuringly. "We have been living here thirty years. It's a great community to be part of. We hate to leave, but Elmer is getting too old to tend to it. We are moving to Florida to be near my sister. Now I hope you and your family are hungry 'cause I'm cooking."

Nancy feared that Dad's wishful thinking of buying a farm—or worse, this farm—was depressingly going to happen. The thought of actually moving away, leaving her friends whom she grew up with, and changing schools was unthinkable. The dreaded thought of just how different, how backward, how corny the high school way out here in the sticks must be was causing her to be on the verge of panic. Her mind was racing now. *Surely Dad will change his mind, and I'll not have to worry about this nightmare.* "I want to go home, Mom," Nancy said as they embraced.

Mom was worried too, but inwardly admired the large yard, the view of the mountain in the background, and the beauty of the surrounding area. She admitted to herself that the scenery was stunningly beautiful. She was getting a picture in her mind of ideas to make some home additions. *Jake said that he was approved on the loan for some improvements, but if he was actually going to go through with this loony idea, a bathroom would be the first order of business—and a kitchen sink too!*

Mom tried to politely decline lunch, but Liz wouldn't hear of it. Elmer, Dad, and I returned after the ride and a tour of the farm. Mom had managed to whisper to Dad that if they stayed for lunch with these strangers, then we would eventually have to use the toilet, which was the outhouse. Dad whispered back and said, "Get used to it, honey. We're buying."

Dad saw all he wanted to see, and he had made his decision. We did stay and eat lunch since Liz went through all the trouble to make it. Dad did not reveal to the Yagers that he had decided to buy, so no negotiations were made. He would handle that through the real estate agent. Mr. Yager said I could go fishing before we left, and I wanted to ride the horse again, but Dad didn't want to seem too anxious in front of the Yagers.

There was a nervous silence for several miles as Dad drove us home. Nancy was despondent because in her mind, her dreams of playing in high school sports, attending class, and graduating with her friends, whom she had known for so long, was ruined. She felt like her life was over.

During the drive, Mom was trying to accept the events of the day. She still didn't understand why the Yagers could live in that house for thirty years without indoor plumbing or toilet. Also, there was only a wood stove for heat. She thought of just how much she loved my dad and his devotion to family, and he really deserved to have this. He had traveled for many years, with his work, and was only home on weekends. It would be wonderful if he could change careers that could allow him to be home nightly. She knew how much this meant to Dad, and he would never give up his dream. She was concerned about Nancy but told herself that everyone would adjust. Mom would just have to deal with her phobia of snakes.

That night, as we all sat at the kitchen table having a snack, Mom told Dad that she supported the move. Dad got up, walked over to where Mom sat, and embraced her. As they hugged, Mom asked, "Didn't Mr. Yager say that his farm is called Circle Y, or something like that?"

"Yeah," Dad laughed. "That name has to go! We're giving the farm our own name. We are going to call it, 'We Found It Ranch,'" Dad announced proudly, "because we found it!"

Mom and I thought the new name was ridiculous at first, but the more we repeated it, the more appropriate it sounded. My parents called the realtor and made an appointment Monday morning to sign a binding contract and mortgage loan application. Nancy, who sat quietly, seemed withdrawn. Finally, she got up, ran to her room, and slammed the door.

Although, I was happy about moving to our new farm, there was one regret that I hadn't considered until it was too late. My best friend, David, and I did everything together. He and I ate school lunches, walked to and from school daily, played sports, hanged out at the playground, had sleepovers, and even visited each other's church often. When I told him the news, I remember he cried. I tried to console him by promising to visit, but I never saw him again.

Nancy was increasingly becoming irritable and distant. My parents assumed it would pass soon enough. Mom assured her that the new location had a great school that could give the students individual attention. "It's a smaller school with smaller class sizes. You will meet new friends, but you can keep the old ones, honey. Stay in contact with them. It's overwhelming at first, but think of it as a new adventure!" Nancy thought otherwise.

"It's going to take time to get a bathroom and kitchen sink, Lily," Dad reasoned. "It will not hurt us to run water from that well and use the outhouse for a while. It'll be good for the kids. They'll have a better appreciation for modern luxuries. It'll be a great experience, and besides, it's only temporary."

"They will have a better appreciation when we have the luxuries installed, you mean. My family is going to wonder about us," Mom said worriedly. "Lisa will think we lost our minds."

"It's not going to kill your sister to shit in an outhouse!" Dad laughed. "I think your family will all get a kick out of visiting us on the farm. Once we are moved in and figure out how much money we'll have, then I'll call the builders and get some prices. Let's not exaggerate. We'll make the best of it. You need to relax, honey."

CHAPTER TWO

THE FOLLOWING MONTH, my parents had the keys to the new home. They sold the old one, and we had to be out of it in one week. We had the daunting task of cleaning the farmhouse and moving all the furniture and our personal belongings. Our goal was to move before the new school year started.

The last day of that week we had all our belongings loaded into a large rental truck and said goodbye to our home of fifteen years. Until then it was the only place my sister and I have ever known. I rode with Dad, who drove the truck. Mom and Nancy took the family car, ahead of us, along with Zoomer. Mom's drive to the farm didn't go well for them. Nancy was miserable. Saying farewell to her friends was harder for her than my parents had anticipated. Of course, the stress of moving, that week, and leaving today, was taking its toll on Mom too. During the two hours of driving, Nancy was too quiet, and when she did speak, she would pick arguments with Mom, who almost backhanded her but managed to gain her composure. It was clear to her that Nancy was going through more than just a young adolescent girl who was angry and upset about relocating. The stark change in her mood, these past few weeks, was getting worse, and Mom was getting really worried.

The outside toilet was another matter awaiting them. Using it daily was the inevitable, and for Mom, nature was calling. On earlier trips to the farm, to prepare the house, she only had to take a quick wheeze in the outhouse, but today, she had to do a number two. She was thankful to have the foresight to place toilet paper in it, on an earlier trip, as she quickly parked the car in the driveway and rushed to the privy. When finishing, she assumed Nancy needed to go too, but would be too squeamish because it would have been her first time using an outside toilet. When Mom opened the door to exit the toilet, she was surprised to see Nancy waiting patiently to use it next. They had survived a small hurdle in their new life.

I was excited about riding Sam as soon as we arrived, but Dad said we must unload the truck first. When we pulled in the driveway, Zoomer was in the yard and was marking his new territory. Mom came out to greet us and to inform Dad about my sister's declining mood.

Unloading the truck was exhausting but still easier and faster than loading it the day before our departure. After we were finishing the last of it, a man who had the appearance of a sharecropper approached. "My name is Everett Reeves. I live on the next place down over there," he pointed. "Always glad to meet new neighbors. Where ya'll from?"

"I'm Jake Johnson and this is my boy, Levi. My wife, Lily, and daughter are inside. We are from Nashville. You lived here long?"

"Violet and me have lived here for a year. She and my boy are back at the house now. He's about your age, young fella. His name is Tommy. Ya'll renting?"

My dad eyed him suspiciously but in response said that we are the new owners. "How about you? Mr. Reaves, is it? Do you own?"

"Call me Everett. Just call me Everett! It's not mine. I work at Bob's Nursery on Highway 55. The nursery owns the house and rents it to me."

Dad observes a trailer next to it. "I see the house. Who lives in the mobile home next to it?"

"My wife's sister and her husband live there. It's small but they'd rather live there than with us. They like their independence. We pulled that trailer all the way from Jackson, where we lived before. Anyway, just wanted to walk over and say howdy."

"You have a kid my age?" I asked.

"Sure do! Come on over and meet him."

"He'll have to make it another day," Dad said. "We need to finish getting moved, now."

I wanted to wait another day to meet Tony too. At that moment, all I could think of was riding my new horse.

We had settled in and prepared to spend our first night on the farm and it was bath time. The Yagers had left behind a small bathtub that appeared to have been made during the Victorian age. Since we had no plumbing yet, we had to draw the water from the well located in the backyard and using a hand crank. Dad was always positive and reminded us that drawing water and using the outhouse was temporary until indoor plumbing was installed.

He also boasted how we were having the opportunity to experience life of a dying era, on a farm.

Mom lay in bed awake that night being thankful that Dad was on vacation next week from his sales management job that required him to be away often overnight. She was not ready to stay at night, in the country, with only Nancy and me. She knew that Dad would return to his work the following week, but she would deal with it then. During Dad's week off, this will allow time to take care of home repairs and painting. Her main concern was my sister's mood issues.

*   *   *   *   *

It was Sunday morning and time for church, although most of the clothes, including our Sunday best, were still packed. We had decided to visit Trinity Baptist, the nearest church from us, and my parents were looking forward to it. They were curious about people in the area too. This was a great way to start our new life.

Leaving our previous church was difficult. My family didn't realize how much we were appreciated until the last Sunday we attended. The pastor stood behind the podium to bid us farewell in our departure in grand fashion. He assured us of the love that the members had for us. Then he surprised us with an announcement of a farewell party that would be held in the reception room immediately after services. The entire church body kept it a secret.

"I'm not going!" Nancy yelled. "I want to go back home! I miss my own room, I miss my friends, I miss my life! I hate both of you!" Mom gave Dad a worried look as she snatched clothes still in the luggage. Dad understood the toll that all of this had on Nancy but had enough of her sass. He stormed toward her room for a showdown that had already been rising to a climax for weeks. Just as he reached for the doorknob, he stopped to think through the best approach and then entered.

"Listen to me, Nancy. What's done is done. You'll make it a lot easier on yourself if you stop fighting it and give this a chance. The only person you are hurting is yourself if you don't try. You will make new friends and you can still keep your old ones. This transition is not easy for your mother and me either. We will help you to adjust if you'll give us a chance, but we will not tolerate your disrespect. You are going to church this morning. Now, get dressed or you are going in those pajamas you're wearing. It's your choice," Dad said sternly to my sister.

Mom was crying when Dad returned to their bedroom. "Oh, Jake, what are we going to do about her?" my mother asked, pleadingly.

"Relax, Lily. I spoke to her. She understood what I said. We will take things one day at a time. Let's visit the new church and see how we like it. It should be interesting. It'll be the first church we have attended, besides our own, in a very long time. Afterward, we'll find a restaurant and relax. This has really been tough the last few days for all of us. We all will take it easy this afternoon. We deserve it."

I wasn't too thrilled about going to church either. Mom just told me that we are going out to eat afterward. I wanted to get back sooner to spend the day riding Sam. I was up early that morning to feed and comb him. Zoomer, in his new pen, was barking wildly. I took a quick look around the barn, out of curiosity, and found some lumber behind it. This gave me the idea to build a tree house. So many things to do today, but Mom said I had to go to church. Just as I started to return to the house, someone from behind me said, "Can we pet Sam?" I turned to see a scruffy-looking boy about my age and an older guy that must have been at least nineteen or twenty years old. "I'm Tommy from the next house, over there," he said as he pointed. "This is my half brother, Larry."

"Sure can. My name is Levi," I replied. "I'm gonna ride him after church. How you know his name is Sam?"

"I know Sam because Mr. Yager has had him for years. I thought he would sell it or something before moving. I've never rode him though. Mr. Yager's wife doesn't like us. She told my pa for us to stay away."

Larry finally spoke up and said, "How old is your sister? What's her name?"

"My sister's name is Nancy. She's fourteen. She doesn't like it here. She didn't want to move here, but I did. There's lots of fun here. I have Sam to ride, we have a pond with lots of fish, and I'm gonna build a tree house and everything," I said excitedly.

Dad peered out the window and walked out of the house to see who I was talking to. "These are the neighbors who live over at that house over there," I said.

"Oh, yes, I met Everett yesterday. You must be his boy," Dad said to Tommy.

"Yeah! How do you like it here?" Tommy asked my dad.

"We're getting settled. I'm Jake." Dad shook Tommy's hand and then reached out to shake Larry's. "Your name?"

"I'm Larry. Everett said ya'll are from the Nashville?"

"Yes, had to get out of the city to have a piece of land of our own in the country. So are you Everett's son too, Larry?"

"No, he's married to my momma. My dad lives in Irving."

"It's good to meet you, but Levi has to come in now and get ready for church. Ya'll come back at another time."

Tommy laughed and said to Larry, "Jerry is not your real dad. He adopted you last year. He's weird."

Larry stared at Tommy with contempt and started to speak, but Dad interrupted and told them to come back a later time. They both walked away quietly, but we could hear them bickering as they approached their home.

"What were they talking about, Dad?" I asked.

"I don't know. Go get ready for church, son."

We entered the church later that morning, as the music was playing and everyone seated. It seemed like the whole congregation took notice of us. The service went normal for a Baptist church. My mind was distracted for I was thinking about all the fun I anticipated back at the farm. I was hoping Zoomer wasn't barking at Sam and making him nervous. The dog was in a much larger pen than the one at our former home. Nancy was withdrawn, which was out of character for her. She was alarmingly becoming the opposite of her usual extroverted demeanor at our former church, or anywhere else in her old life. When we stood up to leave, at the end of the service, several parishioners walked over to greet us. A tall teenage boy said hello to my sister and her eyes brightened.

"His name is Brad, and he's captain of the varsity basketball team, at the high school," Nancy said in the car as the family was leaving church. "He's seventeen and will be a senior. He says he has a car too."

"A car? You and Levi will start school week after next," Dad said. "You'll be making lots of friends."

"It was nice seeing Nancy's spirits lifting this morning," Mom told Dad later, with a sigh of relief. "The boy she met seems like a good kid. Nancy said that his mother is the pianist. I'm so thankful that she has met someone that helps her feel better. Nancy was actually talkative at the restaurant. I think a prayer was answered today."

"I'm thankful too, but not sure I'm ready for my little girl to know senior boys who drive," Dad joked. "She's only fourteen!"

When we returned home, I could finally ride Sam. Dad helped me get it saddled, as Zoomer went crazy with excitement in his pen and was desperate to get out. The pen was barely sturdy enough to hold him in, and Dad said he would rebuild the pen later. Dad wanted to keep Zoomer locked up and not run into the road and hit by a car or stolen.

My sister first noticed Zoomer in a pet store when she was about eight years old. My family had been shopping for a pet, and Nancy begged for the puppy to be allowed out of its cage, to be petted. It was love at first sight, so my parents couldn't resist buying it for her. Nancy even gave our new puppy its name. When we got home, Dad opened the dog cage, and the new puppy ran out and started happily running. "Look at it zoom!" Nancy said. "Let's name it Zoomer!" It's always been Nancy's job to feed and groom him. She took him for walks and trained him to do tricks. Zoomer's care had been part of Nancy's daily routine. However, since the news about us moving, Nancy became not only neglectful in Zoomer's care, but she also stopped showing any affection toward him.

On that Sunday afternoon, the first full day on the farm, as Dad and I were saddling Sam, Nancy ran out the back door to investigate the constant barking. Zoomer had been clawing the ground under the metal dog pen, He managed to crawl under, escape, and run straight toward the horse. It was all Dad could do to hang on to the bridle to keep Sam from running away as the dog was snapping at its legs. Dad yelled at Zoomer to heal. He ran wildly across the yard when he heard Nancy shout to him. Zoomer, excited to be out of the pen and free, eyed a car coming fast down the road. He darted toward the car. The driver had no chance to stop as Zoomer ran under the wheels.

I didn't see the incident or even know what happened at first. I knew something was very wrong when I heard Nancy screeching in terror and a noise that I couldn't identify from the direction of the road on the opposite side of the house. Then my dad said, "I think the dog gotten himself run over." He was in a moment of shock when he saw Nancy run toward the scene and suddenly fall to the ground, shaking uncontrollably. Dad stood over her as her body became momentarily lifeless. He grabbed her, raised her head, and she awakened, disoriented. She began screaming and fighting against Dad's grip and was desperate to run to Zoomer's mangled body. Dad led my sister back to the house to get her away from the site.

Mom ran out of the house, confused and unaware of what happened. She heard Nancy's screams of terror and saw her shaking uncontrollably as Dad held her. In a panic, Mom cried out, "What happened? What's wrong, Jake?"

"The dog ran out in front of a car and Nancy saw it!"

The driver got out of his car and asked, "Is that your dog? I'm sorry I hit it. It ran right out in front of me. I couldn't stop!" We all ignored him as he stood awkwardly at the edge of the road.

Mom howled and she grabbed Nancy to hold her. Nancy was out of control with rage. My parents gave up trying to get her in the house, instead, managed to lay her horizontally on the ground as she twitched and mumbled incoherently.

The death of Zoomer and my sister's setback was heartbreaking. I was only ten, but I realized, along with my parents, how important it was for Nancy to adjust to relocating. My sister's screams terrified me.

Many years later, when Nancy was going through therapy, she would open up and share her nightmares about Zoomer's death. It was the same day and the same events leading to the tragedy. The screech of pain, as she remembered it, was not the same that Zoomer had actually made the second the car struck him. In her dream, the noises Zoomer made were sounds of the damned.

CHAPTER THREE

IT WAS FRIDAY and only two more days until Nancy and I start attending our new school. Everett's wife stopped by to introduce herself. "I'm Violet! I'm sorry about your dog. Folks drive way too fast on this road. Ya'll just got here too."

"Thank you," Mom replied. "Zoomer getting killed is really difficult on my girl, Nancy. She's taking it hard. My name is Lily. Why don't you come in for coffee?"

"Can't stay. Got tomatoes cooking on the stove. Just want to tell ya'll that your younguns will have to catch the bus at the crossroad next to my place. Mr. Jones won't pick 'em up in front of yours. Mr. Jones is the bus driver. They's welcome to wait for the bus at our house on rainy or cold days. They can get on the bus, with my Tommy, right out in front of our place. You meet Tommy. He's about your boy's age. I got another boy. His name is Larry. He's out of school but still lives with us. All of ya'll are welcome to come and see us. If'n you need anythang, just give us a holler. We'ns just country folks."

"Thank you for your kindness," Mom said.

Mom worried that Nancy may not be stable enough to go to school Monday. "She's still not eating good, and is sad all the time. She just stayed in her room with the door closed," Mom said to Dad later that day.

"There will be other dogs. She's going to school, not matter what," Dad replied. "Once she's there and meets new kids, she will be her old self again. She's outgoing and has always loved school. That's not going to change."

Nancy was pale and gaunt when we walked into the church the following Sunday morning, and there was Brad, the boy she had met last Sunday. He was standing at the front corridor, as if he was expecting Nancy to enter. If he noticed that she wasn't her usual self, he certainly didn't show it. Nancy lit up, their eyes locked, and after a moment of awkward greetings, Brad, like a true gentleman, asked my parents if he could sit at the same pew with us. Mom looked at Nancy's expression of approval and said, "Yes, of course." During the service, Brad asked my sister if she could go with him to Loui's, the local burger hangout, but Nancy said she had to ask our parents. Mom approved, desperate to see Nancy lifted from her dark mood, but Dad resisted. When Mom spoke to him privately, he grudgingly went along. A new romance had blossomed, and Mom seemed relieved and hoped this was a means to an end to Nancy's depression.

The following morning, my sister and I walked to the crossroad for our first bus ride to school. As we climbed the bus steps, Mr. Jones introduced himself and said the empty seats will be full by the time we reach the school because there were many more students to pick up. The bus turned the corner and picked up Tommy, who sat next to me. He asked about Zoomer, and if we were going to get another dog. Although we were the same age, he explained how he was "set back" a year due to sickness that kept him out of school for an extended time. However, my dad later commented that the only thing wrong with Tommy is an overprotective mother.

As the students got on, at each stop, many stared at us but few greeted. Finally, one girl, about my sister's age, sat across the aisle from her. "My name is Angie," she said and smiled as she spoke to Nancy, who murmured a hello. "You just moved here?" Nancy replied that she had. "Welcome to Morris! I been living here all my life." Nancy seemed to like Angie. After the next few stops, Angie's friend, Lucy, got on and sat in the middle seat that Angie was saving and the three got acquainted. I heard Angie shout, "You went out with Brad Simon, yesterday?" Then I heard all three whisper and giggle.

Ricky Dawson was my first acquaintance, after Tommy, who sat on the row in front of us. Ricky and I discovered that we lived within walking distance, but it didn't seem like that at first. After I got on the bus, it winded around the backroads for twenty minutes or so in a big circle, until we ended up almost where we started where Ricky got on. We were in the same grade, we both collected model cars and baseball cards, and I invited Ricky over to fish in our pond. I don't recall how we got on the subject of church, but he asked if my family attended. I told him we were Baptist. His response to my answer was not only surprising but was offensive and diminished any close friendship that we could have had. "We don't believe in ya'll," was the comment he made. This was my first exposure of conflict that divides some church denominations, especially in smaller Southern towns and communities.

The school was two unimpressive, small, old buildings and all twelve grades were located on the same grounds. One of the buildings held grades seven through twelve, and the other was the elementary school. I was starting grade six and the entire sixth grade body of about twenty-five was in one room. The late August Tennessee heat made the room feel like an oven. The stiff material of my new denim jeans was sticking to my legs as the morning wore on. The starch in my new shirt, against my neck, felt almost unbearable. The teacher, Mrs. Grizzle, asked the class if there were any new students who had relocated from another school since last year, to raise our hand. Since I was the only one, she asked me to stand before the class and introduce myself. Although I was embarrassed to do this, it helped to break the ice and to feel more comfortable with the other classmates, to my surprise. Decades later, I reconnected with some of the students that I met my first year at the Morris school through the social network of Facebook.

When getting off the bus that afternoon, I couldn't wait to shed my stiff new jeans and starched shirt. Nancy seemed to fair quiet well for her first day in a new school, for several students said bye to her, until tomorrow, as she exited the bus. With all she had been through with moving and the loss of her beloved Zoomer, she hasn't lost her gift to connect and be the envy of the other kids. However, there was something different. Something about her that was not right. Something within her that's dark and ominous and it chilled our mother.

It was Dad's last evening of his vacation. He took one more day off to get settled. Tomorrow, he would be away, on his sales route, until Friday night. Mom was worried about us being alone all week in the country. He assured her that the area was safe and if there was a problem, then the sheriff is not far away. He also said that he had a lead on a new job that would allow him to be home nightly and Mom couldn't have been happier about that. Dad was hopeful too. He was becoming tired of his current job as a sales manager, and besides, the sales line was phasing out. The salesmen that he managed sold household products to residents on their weekly sales routes. More and more people were buying these items at various stores, sprouting up in rural areas.

The next morning, the wind was up, and the weather was beginning to look nasty as my sister and I was walking to the corner to catch the bus. Mom came outside, shouting for us to stop so she could give us an umbrella, out of concern, that it would rain before the bus arrived. As we waited, Tommy shouted from his doorsteps, inviting us to wait inside his house. Nancy recalled Tommy's mother, Violet, talking to Mom and the offer that we could wait inside her place anytime and catch the bus that stops in the front. Nancy spoke up and replied that we would think about it, but when it was starting to seriously rain, together we made a dash to Violet's house. We knocked and Violet cracked the front door open and said to wait a second, then we heard what sounded like her in a hushed but stern tone. She seem to be disciplining someone, and we heard a scornful male voice. Tommy finally opened the door for us to enter. Tommy's older half brother, Larry, was wearing only pants, his belt unbuckled and no shirt. There was also an older man, who was much taller and bigger, that seemed to be in his thirties. He was wearing an unbuttoned shirt and boxer shorts. He quickly walked away when we came in, but Larry looked awkwardly at Nancy with an embarrassed expression. He was hastily trying to fold up a rollaway bed that was in the center of the front room.

Larry introduced himself to Nancy and asked us both to sit. The older man returned a couple of minutes later, fully dressed, and introduced himself as Jerry.

"This is my dad," Larry added.

Nancy, who had always been straightforward, snickered and asked, "Do you always sleep with your dad?"

"Just when he comes here for a visit. We don't have an extra bed. He lives in town, and he visits here when he can."

"Why don't you live with him at his house?" Nancy asked.

"My mama lives here, so I live with her."

"How old are you, Larry"?

"I'm nineteen."

"Your dad looks so young."

"He adopted me," Larry said. I remember Tommy commented that Larry had been adopted, about two years ago or so, as I told Nancy later on the bus. We both thought it was a very peculiar thing.

The bus stopped to pick up Ricky, and he sat with me again. I told Dad about his remark about not believing in the church that we attended. Dad asked about the church Ricky attended, which was Church of Reverence. Dad instructed me on how to reply to the remark next time I saw Ricky.

"You said that you don't believe in the church my family and me attended, remember?" I asked Ricky.

"Yeah," Ricky said with a surprised expression.

"Well, does the church you attend believe that Christ is your savior?"

"Yeah."

"The church I attend believes this too. Does the church you attend believe that Christ died on the cross so that our sins will be forgiven?"

"Yeah."

"The church I attend believes this too. There is no reason that we cannot respect each church we attend." This ended the discussion, and Ricky made no more comments about my family's church affiliation.

Nancy quickly became very popular in her class because of her own personality. She had always excelled socially, and she was dating Brad, the most popular guy in school. It seemed that her bout with depression was finally ending for good. She was recovering from the loss of Zoomer and adjusting to the family's new life, including her new school. Mom continued to watch my sister closely. She thought back in time to Nancy's reaction to their pet's death and her brooding over moving away.

"A bunch of us are gonna stay at my house, Friday night. You should come too, Nancy. It's gonna be a gas!" Angie said as the girls ate in the school lunchroom.

"Friday night? I'll talk to my mother. My dad will be getting home late that night. He'll be gone all week. She might not let me go unless he's home too, but I'll tell her. How many will be there?"

"Well, there's Lucy, Judy, Lynn, Anne, and maybe Wanda and Teresa. Momma and I are making sandwiches, and we'll have potato chips and soda pop. All of ya'll can bring any kind of food you like."

"Do you have a record player? I'll bring all my albums!"

"I have a Magnavox player with AM/FM radio. I got it for Christmas a couple of years ago. I just bought Bob Dylan's *Highway 61* album and The Beatles' new album, *Help!* Both of these were just released last month. Lucy has lots of singles that she'll bring. We are gonna have a ball!"

"Will your parents be there?"

"Yeah, but it's okay. My parents won't go ape over it, even if we can stay up all night!"

"What time should I be at your house?"

"Well, it'll start around six. We'll need time to make all the food, after I get home from school, but you can get off the bus with me and help us, if you would like, Nancy."

"Did you tell Nancy about the sleepover Friday?" Lucy asked Angie as she joined them and sat at the lunch table. "I'm making rice krispie cookies to bring."

"We're talking about it now. My mamma doesn't want a bunch of grody dishes," Angie said. "Can you bring paper plates and cups, Lucy?"

"Sure. Here comes Julie."

"Hey everybody," said Julie as she sat with the others.

"This is Nancy Johnson, Julie. She moved from Nashville over the summer."

"Hi, Nancy. Aren't you dating Brad Simon?"

"Yeah. He's nice," Nancy responded.

"He's a doll," Angie chimed in as the three rose from the table to go to their classes.

Nancy just had to go to that party Friday night. The thought of Mom not allowing it first caused panic, then anger, that she was trying to conceal from new friends. Her mind racing, she shoved aside a student, who unintentionally blocked her path, as her puzzled classmates looked on.

Nancy's mind was distracted much of the day after lunch hour. She thought about Brad and the party this Friday night. *Brad has so much more going for him than any guy she had met*, she thought. *He introduced me to his parents. Most guys won't do that. He's so mature. I feel safe when I'm with him. He is the only thing in my life that makes me happy. He will eventually visit our house, and he'll find out that we have no indoor bathroom and must get our water from a well in the backyard. That's going to be so embarrassing. When I talked to him after lunch, he said he and his friends will come to Angie's Friday night. Mom just has to let me go to it and stay the night. She may not want me to because Dad will be home late that night. If I tell her there may be other girls who will stay overnight and that Brad, along with other boys, will be there too, then I know she will make me stay at home. I've got to go there no matter what and see Brad. I'll just tell Mom that it will be only Angie and me.*

At the same period that Nancy and her new friends were having lunch, Brad was in geometry class, daydreaming. *Nancy is very beautiful. She's different than any girl I've ever met. When I was trying to find the nerve to ask her out, she must have known. She started to flirt, and it helped talking to her a lot easier. I really like the way she talks and the funny things that she says. She cracks me up the way she tells a story and acts out the voices of people. When we were at the diner, she impersonated our pastor so well, and it made me laugh so hard that my soda came out my nose. I was embarrassed, but she wasn't grossed out. She thought it was funny. I heard that she's going to Angie's party Friday night. Angie said that it's okay for some of the guys to stop by, but not too late. I'll be there.*

*　*　*　*　*

The morning my dad had gone back to work, after his vacation, he had a job interview at a local utility company. He didn't tell my mom about the appointment for not disappointing her if he failed to get the position. He was jubilant with excitement when he called my mom to tell her he got the job. "Guess what, honey? You are talking to the new supplies manager for Jackson's Utility!" Dad announced to Mom over the telephone.

"Are you serious? Are you telling me the truth, Jake?" Mom asked excitedly.

"I start week after next. That's when Mr. Hunter, the personnel manager, would like me to start. I've already gave notice."

"Why didn't you tell me earlier?"

"I wanted it to be a surprise. Besides, I really didn't think there would be much of a chance of getting a position like this. I found the job listing in the Nashville paper two weeks ago. I get a pay raise, and I'm home every night and I'm off most weekends!"

"Oh, Jake, I bet Bob is really upset with you. He gave you your start, as manager, with Ace Home Service. You and he are such good friends! Have you talked to him yet?"

"No, not yet. I just mailed my resignation last night to him. It'll take three days to reach his office. My last day to work will be next Friday, so to be fair, I wired him this morning since I have given a short notice."

"What if things don't work out with this new company? Then what would we do?"

"Relax, honey," Dad assured Mom. "I was their top route manager last year, remember? I'll know, quick enough, if it's not going to pan out, and I'm sure I'll get my job back, if it doesn't, but it will. I wouldn't be taking this step if I wasn't sure. I've been checking out this new position for a while. It's going to work. The time has come to leave Ace. I've been with the company for fifteen years and it's time to leave."

"You'll really be home every night, Jake, and weekends off?"

"Most weekends off. There will be some Saturdays and even Sundays that I'll have to go in for yearend audits or when there is a problem. I will have to travel overnight now and again for some training. I will be visiting other company branches, but typically, it's a home-every-night and weekends-off job. After fifteen years with Ace, being away almost every day, I wouldn't have it any other way."

"Well, when you get home this weekend, we must celebrate! This is such great news, Jake. I must tell you that I got a letter from Lisa. She and George will be here next Saturday. I look forward to seeing my sister and with you getting this new job. I'm just beside myself. I feel blessed! Oh honey, I can't wait for you to get home. It seems we have been through so much while moving here, and I'm so worried about Nancy. She's just not been herself. I've been dreading you going back to your sales route after your vacation ended. I haven't been looking forward to being here, in the country, with just the kids and me all by ourselves."

"Now Lily, as I told you before, the sheriff knows ya'll are home alone. You have his number and he's not far away. I also told Everett, and he said he will look after things and that ya'll can count of them anytime. Just keep your doors locked at night. We live in a very low-crime area. I'll call again later this week to check on you. I'll be home late Friday night. I have one more week and I'm done with Ace. Just sit tight and relax."

"I'll try. I'm going to call Lisa this evening and find out what time they'll be here and just talk to her."

"Be sure and tell George to bring his fishing gear. He'll love riding Sam too. So will Lisa!"

"Oh Jake, I can't imagine my sister getting on a horse. I'll send them your love!"

"I have to get back to work. I'll call later this week. I love you and bye-bye."

"I love you too and be careful driving. Call me later this week."

*　　*　　*　　*　　*

Nancy was getting nervous when she arrived home after school. "I must persuade Mom to let me go to the party, Friday night," she thought. "I'll just pretend it's no big deal and she will surely be okay with it. She'll be scared to be alone with just Levi, but I'll convince her that nothing will happen." Nancy was shaking as she opened the door to confront Mom.

"Hi, Mom!"

"How was school?"

"It was okay. It's a lot different from my old school."

"Where is your brother?"

"He's in the back to check on that horse. Hey, Mom, my new friend, Angie, that I told you about wants me to stay at her house this Friday night."

"This Friday? I don't know about that, Nancy. You just met her. You know nothing about her family."

Nancy wasn't expecting this response. "Oh, Mom, please? It's going to be okay. Her parents will be there. It's just for one night and I like her. She doesn't live far from here. You won't have to drive me there. I'm just going to get off the bus at her house. She said that her mom will drive me home the next day."

Mom pondered the thought. She was pleased with Nancy's progress with dealing with her melancholy, and she deserved to have some fun. She knew that she should really discuss this with Dad, though, but she'll tell him when he calls later this week.

"I'll feel better if I drive you there to meet her and her parents. Better yet, I want to meet her mother today or tomorrow, or at least speak with her on the telephone. What is your friend's number?" Mom asked.

Nancy at first began to panic at the thought of Mom's request. If she knew other girls would be staying overnight at Angie's, then she surely would not allow Nancy to spend the night. Her panic turned into inner rage, which she desperately suppressed. If Mom called Angie's mother, then she will know that other girls will be staying over. Maintaining her composure, she told Mom not worry.

"I will feel better about you staying the night in a strange home if I could talk to your friend's mother. I know nothing about them, and frankly, you don't either," Mom insisted.

"I can take care of myself. I can't believe you don't trust me! I just want to spend the night with my new friend! What's the big deal?" Nancy exclaimed.

My mom, fearful that my sister may be on the verge of a setback with her emotions, chose her words carefully. "You can spend the night with your friend, Nancy. I still want her telephone number in case I need to get ahold of you for any reason, okay?" She suspected Nancy was hiding something. There was a look of raw hatred in Nancy's eyes that was unsettling, but she wasn't going surrender to Nancy's resistance. After several seconds of awkward silence, she finally said, "Please get her telephone number for me later, okay, honey?" Nancy glared at her but said nothing.

Surprisingly, Angie's mother, Judy, called my mom, later that same afternoon. After the greetings and a few pleasantries, Judy welcomed our family to the area. "You and your family are going to love it here. I understand that you are city folks. I've lived here all of my life. You will not find nicer people than here in Morris."

"Thank you for having Nancy for the sleepover Friday," Mom said.

"It's a pleasure, Lily. Angie says some wonderful things about your daughter. They get along very well. You bought Mr. Yager's place, correct? The Circle Y Ranch, is it?"

"Yes, we did. We just moved in. It has a new name now. It's called the 'We Found It Ranch.' That's the name my husband came up with."

"That's an interesting name," said Judy. "I like it! It's catchy!" After both had a good laugh, she said, "My husband, Pete, and I will be home. All the girls can all sleep over, and we will make sure they are in bed before midnight. Angie has had these before, so I know what to expect."

All the girls? Nancy, didn't say there would be more girls staying over. "Why would Nancy not mention it? This must be what she is hiding and hesitant to give me Angie's phone number for fear I would know that it would be more than just the two. This is not like her. Mom was curious to know how many planned to spend the night, so she asked Judy.

"There will be about six to eight in total, but don't worry, they're all good girls. They'll have fun. They always do. If you're worried, you are welcome to stop by for a visit Friday evening and meet Angie and the other girls. It'll give us a chance to get acquainted too."

"I told my girl that I'll drive her there. She's really excited about it. I'll come in for a few minutes. I look forward to meeting you."

After the telephone conversation with Judy, Mom was troubled about Nancy's deception. She thought about the best way to confront her, considering my sister's nervousness. However, Nancy, who was eavesdropping from the next room, burst into the room. Her face seemed distorted as she loudly cursed Mom. "How dare you spy on me How dare you, how dare you, how dare you!"

"Levi, go to your room now and shut the door!" Mom instructed. "I don't want you hearing this." I'm sitting on the couch, but I don't move. She repeated, "Levi, go to your room, now!" Nancy began to cry, hysterically. I did as Mom said, and I closed the door, but I put my ear against its surface and could hear every word. "Nancy, what in the world has gotten into you? You have never talked like this before!"

"You are what's gotten in to me! You and Dad! He moved us to this stupid house, in this stupid hick town, to a stupid hick school and you just let him do it! You could have stopped him! He just leaves all week and we have to live in this hole. He's always gone and don't you realize that Zoomer would be alive if we hadn't moved? It's all his fault and it's all your fault! Do you realize that?" Mom attempted to speak, but Nancy shouted her down. "Do you realize that I have nightmares every night! Every night! *Every night!* And why are you spying on me!" Nancy fell to the floor, curled into a fetal position, and went into to hysterics.

Mom gently put her arm around Nancy. Her only thought was to help Nancy calm down. For the moment, it's all that mattered. Mom continued to hold her. Nancy was motionless and she remained in the same position for five long minutes before finally speaking. "Mommy, I'm sorry Mommy." She spoke like a small child. "I didn't mean it. I just really want to be with my new friends. You'll not let me, now. Lots of girls will be there, so you won't let me go, now." Nancy began to cry again.

Nancy remained quiet as Mom held her for several moments and finally spoke in a calm voice. "Oh, honey, of course you can be with your new friends. We want you to have friends. Angie's mother called me. Surely, you heard the phone ring. It's all going to be okay, honey." They were caressing while slowing rocking and comforting each other.

Nancy spoke in a normal voice, now. "Mom . . . Mom . . . I'm sorry . . . please believe me . . . I'm sorry I said those things. Please don't tell Dad. I don't know what's happening to me. I don't feel right anymore. I'm having horrible dreams at night. I'm not sleeping well. I don't want to sleep anymore. Those dreams . . . those dreams! I can't take it anymore!"

"Tell me about your dreams, honey,"

"Zoomer . . . Zoomer . . . the sounds . . . those sounds . . . I can't . . . I *can't!* I can't tell you! It's too horrible!"

"It's okay, honey. Don't try to tell me. Try not to think about the dreams. Just relax."

Mom was racking her brain on what to do or say next. She decided to switch to another subject, unrelated to Zoomer, or relocating. "Tell me about Brad, honey. You like him?"

After a few seconds, Nancy responded. "Yeah, I do." Then she begins to stutter. "I-I-I really do and d-d-don't want to lose h-h-him. Oh Mom, I'm so scared."

"Nancy, honey. I see how Brad looks at you in church. I really don't think he'll leave you." Mom knew that my sister's self-esteem was not what it once was. She had changed from the confident girl who had few worries with a strong command of her peers and especially the boys. Then she remembered the talk she had with Dad earlier. "Nancy, honey, I have good news about your dad's work. He found a new job working locally, and he'll be home every night. He starts next Monday. I'm so happy about it."

"W-w-where? W-w-what type of work will he do? He'll be home every night?"

"He'll be a manager at the local utility company and be home every evening."

"I don't hate him . . . and I don't hate you, Mom."

CHAPTER FOUR

D AD CALLED HOME again, as promised, on Friday morning. Mom was thrilled to hear his voice. "How has your week been, honey?" Dad asked.

"Oh, Jake, I'm so worried about Nancy. She had another crying fit."

Mom told Dad about Nancy's overnight party with her girlfriends. She told how she was distraught with fear at the chance that Mom would not allow her to go. Mom did as she had promised Nancy and said nothing to him about Nancy's profanity.

"Crying fit? Another one, over something like that?" Dad asked. "That girl has got to get ahold of herself. Levi didn't see all of this, did he?"

"I sent him to his room, but he heard it, but he's okay. My main worry is about Nancy. I spoke to the girl's mother, who is having the party, and she and her husband will be there and make sure all the girls don't stay up all night. She said I could be there too if I want too. Actually, I think it will be good for Nancy. She needs to start having fun and see what the new community has to offer and have new friends."

"I'm going to talk to her this weekend and see what's going on with her. She should be adjusting to the move and the new school."

"We should look for a new dog. It's traumatized her so much seeing Zoomer get ran over. I think she has been having bad dreams about that, but she will not tell me too much."

"We'll see. I'll be home before midnight, I hope."

"I miss you, Jake. Did you talk to your boss about leaving?"

"Yeah. When he read my wire about resigning, he told his wife that he was going out for a drink." He laughed.

"That's not a surprise. I know he must be very upset."

"I'll tell you all about it when I get home. I miss you too. I miss all of you. I can't wait to get home. This week has been a strain on both of us."

Mom dragged me along that Friday afternoon to Angie's house. Nancy seemingly overcame her emotional outburst and was anxious about the fun night with her new girlfriends. Next to me in the back seat was apple pie, potato chips, and tuna sandwiches, to offer as a contribution to my sister's pajama party, or whatever they wanted to call it. We were greeted warmly by Angie's mother, Judy, who gave my mom assurance of Nancy's safety. She again invited us to stay the evening until the girls would finally wear themselves out. Mom said that we can just stay a short time because we were expecting Dad to return home after working and on the road all week.

About eight girls were there, including Angie and Nancy. There was also Lucy, Julie, Lynn, Anne, Wanda, and Theresa. All brought a variety of snacks. In addition to the sandwiches that Angie and Nancy provided, there was also pigs-in-a-blanket, onion dip, rice krispie cookies, and ice cream. They wasted little time cranking up the Magnavox stereo with records and albums by the Animals, Herman's Hermits, the Beach Boys, Tom Jones, Sam the Sham, the Byrds, and the Moody Blues, while dancing and laughing. As the night wore on, they had plans to do crazy makeovers, play some board games, spin the bottle, and cup stacking. It was almost eight o'clock when the doorbell rang. When Angie opened the front door, standing nervously was Brad with Ted and Johnny, two of his buddies. The music started again as Brad and Nancy embraced as if they were long, lost lovers. Ted paired with Angie, and Johnny made eye contact with Lucy. All were dancing and talking.

"Angie, the boys will have to leave by ten o'clock. House rules!" Judy announced to her daughter when she entered the room. "You boys are invited to eat before you go. We have plenty, but you must leave us by ten, okay?"

"There's no school, tomorrow! Please, Momma, let them stay until eleven," Angie protested.

"Now, I've talked to your friends' parents, and all of them were okay with the boys being here, but they all agreed that they should be gone by ten. Case closed."

"Can I see you tomorrow, Nancy?" Brad asked.

Considering her earlier outburst in front of Mom earlier, Nancy was doubtful that she could go out with Brad. Besides, Dad would be coming home tonight and will want us all to be together tomorrow. "I'll ask," she replied.

"I'll see you Sunday morning, at church, at least?"

"I look forward to it, Brad."

After the boys left, the girls had a game of spin the bottle and talked about old and new crushes. Then they started rating all the other students they knew at school. One girl turned the television on and an old movie about witches. It was turned low and they flipped the lights off to scare each other with horror stories.

"Did anyone see the newspaper article about the bell witch?" Julie asked everyone. "It's a true story that happened over a hundred years ago. A family was haunted by a witch!"

"I read it, but I don't believe it." Lynn laughed.

"I heard about it," Lynn added. "I heard that some people have stood in front of a mirror and closed their eyes, spin around three times, while repeating, 'I believe in the bell witch,' and a witch appeared in the mirror!"

"Let's try it!" said Angie.

"That's too scary," said Lucy.

"Oh, come on," Angie insisted. "I'll go first."

"I think it'll be fun," Annie finally joined in. "You do it first, Angie, then I'll go next. We'll all take turns!"

All the girls congregated in the bathroom that was larger than most. So that all could fit in, two stood in the bathtub to observe Angie, who stood in front of mirror. For effects, she lit a candle on the sink and turned off the ceiling light before the game began to summon the bell witch.

"Remember to close your eyes, spin around three times, while repeating, 'I believe in the bell witch,'" Lynn reminded Angie.

Angie closed her eyes and slowly turned while repeating, "I believe in the bell witch." She turned slowly again and once more repeated, "I believe in the bell witch." One last time, she repeated, "I believe in the bell witch," while turning a full turn. She opened her eyes and saw her own image in the mirror, as all the girls giggled.

"Annie, you're next," said Angie, laughing.

Annie stood nervously in front of the mirror, closed her eyes, and repeated the words, "I believe in the bell witch" each of the three times she turned. Then Wanda was next, but she and Annie saw nothing but their own image and the reflection of the other girls who were observing. Lucy, Julie, and Lynn followed, each repeating the words while turning three times, with the same results. Theresa's overactive imagination got the best of her, so she backed away and flatly refused to participate. This left Nancy, who was inwardly overwhelmed with fright and would rather have a needle stuck in her eye than to take part in this. However, she was struggling to regain her once superior social standing among peer groups. Her mind had wandered back to the time when she radiated confidence.

"Nancy? Nancy? Are you there?" asked Angie. Nancy pulled her mind to the present moment. "You were a million miles away!" The others were laughing, but she said nothing and stood in front of the mirror.

Nancy closed her eyes and after several seconds, the other girls coaxed her to turn and repeat the chant. She turned clockwise slowly and said, "I believe in the bell witch." She turned again. "I believe in the bell witch." She turned for the third and final time. "I b-b-believe in the bell witch."

She opened her eyes. In the reflection was an image not of herself. The eyes were blood red and piercing into Nancy's with contempt. The skin was covered with blisters and deep wrinkles and was the color of death. The image in the reflection, where Nancy's should have been, had long white hair that was floating. It extended its hand that penetrated through the mirror as if it intended to touch her. The image opened its mouth that showed dozens of long and pointed teeth. The words that it spoke haunted Nancy until the day she died. It was as if two voices from hell were speaking in unison. It said, "Take my hand, Nancy, and come with me."

Out of unspeakable fear as to what could happen if she disobeyed the commandment, Nancy extended her own hand. Angie grabbed her and shouted, "What's wrong, Nancy!" The other girls trembled at Nancy's bloodcurdling screams.

*   *   *   *   *

Mom stayed up to wait for Dad to return home. She was startled when the telephone rang late that evening. "Mrs. Johnson? Is this Mrs. Johnson?"

"Who is this?" she replied.

"This is Pete Drake, Angie's father. Mrs. Johnson, your daughter fainted. You need to come here immediately!"

"What? Fainted?"

"The girls were playing a game and something scared her. She's awake now and lying on the couch."

"Oh my God! I'll be right there!" She hung up the telephone and awakened me. "Get up, Levi! Something happened to Nancy!"

Julie's mother was waiting for us at her front door when we arrived. "She's doing better now. She seems terrified."

"Why? What happened?" Mom demanded as we were climbing the porch steps.

"The girls were playing a harmless game about summoning a witch," Judy replied. "Nancy screamed and fell to the floor. She was shaking and her eyes were rolled back. We finally were able to help her up and walk her to the couch."

Nancy was still lying on the couch when Mom reached her. "I want to go home," Nancy said.

"What happened, Nancy? Tell me what you saw." Nancy's eyes had a blank stare and she said no more. Mom and Judy each grabbed her arms and helped her to sit upright then helped her to our car.

When we arrived home, Dad's car was in the driveway. "Thank God your dad is home," Mom said in relief. We had rushed out of the house earlier after getting the call from Judy and didn't leave a note for Dad. Mom tried to coax Nancy out of the car, but she wouldn't respond. She just sat on the passenger side with a blank stare. "Stay with your sister, Levi, while I go get your Dad." Mom hurried inside the house, and moments later both she and Dad came running out.

"Nancy . . . Nancy!" my dad called, but she wouldn't answer my dad so he picked her up out of the car and carried her inside the house and laid her on her bed.

After several moments, Nancy snapped out of her apparent trance and look around, and she was confused. She whispered, "M-m-mommy?"

"What happened, sweetie?" Mom asked.

"I saw a b-b-bad lady."

"Who is the bad lady, honey?" Dad asked.

"In the mirror! S-s-she was coming out of the mirror!" Nancy screeched in sheer terror.

Mom and Dad left the room to talk in private. "What in the world went on in that house?" Dad asked Mom.

"Julie, Angie's mother, said the girls were just playing a harmless game about that bell witch thing. The Drakes seem like very normal people. I talked to the other girls who were there, and they all said there was nothing there that would scare her. She just started screaming. It's so strange. Nancy called me Mommy, and in a little girl's voice. She did the same earlier this week when she became very upset. Her nervousness is getting worse, Jake."

"I'm calling those people right now and get to the bottom of this. What's the phone number?"

Pete answered when Dad called. "This is Jake Johnson, Nancy's father. Is this Mr. Drake?"

"Yeah, this is Pete Drake. Angie and her friends shouldn't have been trying to conjure up a witch. That's a dangerous game. How is your daughter?"

"She's terrified! Do you think that any of these girls could have slipped my daughter dope?"

"Absolutely, no. I know these girls and I know my daughter."

"Someone must have been playing a prank then."

"Look, Mr. Johnson, nobody was doing that. I've talked to all who were here, and they all said there was nothing out of line. I do think they should not have been playing any witch game. I can understand how a young girl's imagination can be exaggerated while playing such a game, but no one was messing around with a prank. How is she doing now?"

"She's resting. Thanks for looking after her."

"Sure, Mr. Johnson. Let us know how she's doing."

"Good night, Mr. Drake."

*　　*　　*　　*　　*

Sunday morning, Nancy was still in her bedroom at breakfast time. She was in a zombielike state when Mom checked on her. She was sitting on the edge of her bed, staring into space. "Tell me about what happened last night, honey?" Mom asked, but Nancy said nothing. "Why don't you come to breakfast? You need to eat. It'll make you feel better." Nancy's eyes met Mom's with a cold stare that made her flinch. My sister stayed in her room the entire day.

Overnight, party lines buzzed with small-town gossip throughout the community over the "witch" incident at last night's party. Sunday morning, we got up to attend church as if things were normal. Mom went into Nancy's room to have her get dressed, fearful of leaving her home alone. She balked but managed to pull herself together with the incentive to meet Brad at church but worried that he didn't call the day before.

Mom noticed dark areas under Nancy's eyes; otherwise she looked okay. Our family walked into the church and down the middle aisle that divided the two columns of pews. It seemed that all eyes were on Nancy. Brad, who anticipated meeting Nancy at church, glanced over from where he was sitting but made no move to walk over to greet Nancy.

Brad was exceptionally fond of Nancy until he heard about the weird story of her imagining seeing a witch. *This is all too creepy for me,* he thought. *I see her walking in now. I'll pretend I don't see her. The whole church knows about this. The entire school knows about this. I can't be seen with someone like that. Only a crazy person would see witches in a mirror.*

Nancy saw Brad quickly glance at her. *He knows I'm here, but he's not coming over like he promised Friday night. He didn't even nod at me. He's totally ignoring me.* Brad's reaction left Nancy in quiet despair.

Mom and Dad, too, noticed that Brad had snubbed Nancy and started to ask her if there was something wrong between the two, but decided to let it go. Since the incident Friday night at the party, it was easy to put two and two together.

After the church service, Brad avoided eye contact with Nancy as he rushed out a side door. Not wanting to embarrass Nancy over her rejection from Brad, my parents didn't bring it up on the ride home from church. They decided to talk with her later, in private. Nancy, again, was quiet and withdrawn. Once we pulled into the driveway, Nancy rushed out of the car and straight to her bedroom. She stayed in there all afternoon, refusing to come out or discuss the matter with my parents.

*   *   *   *   *

Everett and Violet didn't attend church, but they did conduct living-room prayer meetings Sunday mornings. Violet's sister, June, and her husband, Johnny, who lived in the trailer next door, usually joined in on the "house church." "Looks like the devil got his hold on that poor child," Violet said. "Satan possessed her with evil spirits!"

"Now, Violet! Let it be. That's just gossip," Everett pleaded.

Violet ignored Everett and held up her Bible, while looking upward and shouting, "Lawd, deliver that child from evil spirits and guard her against the devil's scheming ways. We bow before you, Lawd, that the devil be cast out of that child's soul. Aaaaamen."

"Nancy didn't see the devil, Ma. She seen a witch in a mirror," Tommy explained.

"It's all the devil's doings, Tommy. You be respectin' our prayer time, now," Violet said sternly.

The following Monday morning, Mom called and notified the school that Nancy would not be attending due to a doctor's appointment, since her situation was getting worse. "It could be physical," Dad guessed. "She could have epilepsy or something like that. We will get her checked out and hope for the best. This is my last week on the job so I'm calling off today. We'll both talk to the doctor and get to the bottom of things. All of this with Nancy has gone far enough."

"Epilepsy? Oh, dear God, no!" Mom said uneasily.

After I got on the school bus, Mr. Jones turned the corner and stopped to pick up Tommy. Violet stepped outside and motioned to go on without Tommy. I remembered he said that he was set back a grade for missing school due to sickness. He must be working on another grade setback. Poor Tommy. Ricky, the boy who made the crack about my family's church faith, sat on the row of seat across from me. He looked over and said, "I heard your sister had an attack." Not knowing exactly how to respond to Ricky's question but wanting to defend my sister, I just said that someone was playing a joke on her.

"I heard she went nuts and thought she saw a witch in a mirror. Where is she now?" Ricky said.

His remark enraged me so much that without giving it any thought, I slammed his head with my biology textbook. Mr. Jones's instantly slammed on the brakes and ordered us to sit separated from each other until we arrive at the school. When we were finally there, neither one of us would talk about the excursion with Jones. He let the incident go with a warning.

Throughout the school day, a couple of other students asked about my sister but were kinder about their comments. I was thankful when the school day ended.

My parents were in Dr. Harris's office and sat across his desk after Nancy's exam. "Mr. and Mrs. Johnson, physically, your daughter is healthy. It's possible she had developed an overactive imagination over the weekend festivities that we discussed. I think the recent nervousness and melancholy were derived from relocating from another school. Also, the shock of witnessing the family pet getting hit by an automobile. Such events can trigger temporary psychosis. You are smart to bring her in while in its early stages. I am prescribing her benzodiazepine. This should help keep her calm. Make sure she sees me in one week." Such medicine, a year later, would remind me of Jagger belting out a tune called "Mother's Little Helper." What a gas.

Mom wasted no time making sure Nancy took a pill with water when we arrived home. It seemed to work. She was actually smiling a little and talking a while afterward. My parents were discussing privately in their bedroom about Nancy's plight while she and I sat on the front porch. Larry, Tommy's half brother, and Jerry, whom Larry claimed was his stepfather, were walking by. I shouted to them and they stopped and waved.

"Where are you two going?" Nancy asked as she snickered.

"We're just taking a stroll," Jerry replied.

"You been riding your horse any, Levi?" Larry asked me.

"Almost every day!" I replied. "Sam threw me off the first time I rode him, but I didn't let that happen again . . ."

Nancy interrupted, looked at Jerry with a smirk, and asked, "Did you really adopt Larry?"

"Yes," was Jerry's only reply.

"How do ya'll like living here?" Larry asked, trying to change the subject.

"I like it 'cause I can have a horse, and we have a large pond with lots of fish. There's plenty of space to ride my bike too!" I said.

"Your little brother said he adopted you just a year ago," Nancy said as she glared at Larry. "You're a little old to be adopted, don't you think?"

Jerry was nudging at Larry, trying to force him to ignore the exchange and keep walking. "It was longer than a year ago," Jerry spoke up. "Let's go, Larry."

"It was three years ago," Larry said sharply.

"Well, I think you two are really hump buddies. Isn't that right?"

"That is not something to discuss with a young girl! Let's keep walking, Larry," Jerry said crossly.

Yep. I think that pill that my parents gave Nancy helped her to open up and return to her old self, at least for the moment. Welcome back, Nancy.

CHAPTER FIVE

BERNICE CALDWELL HAD just become a new subscriber to the multiparty telephone line that was shared by a group of other subscribers. It was a new passion for Bernice to call her best friend, Penny Vickers, every morning, for two hours or more sometimes. Since only one subscriber at a time could use their phone, they would have to make their calls before or after Bernice tied it up. It seems that she and Penny loved nothing more than to gossip on the party line and anyone in the group could eavesdrop. All they had to do was pick up their telephone receiver and listen.

"Did you see that slutty dress that Bonnie had on in church Sunday morning?" asked Bernice.

"Sure did, and she's so stuck up she'd drown in a rainstorm!" replied Penny. "Did you see Gary Ross? I could smell liquor on his breath!"

"He goes to Charlie's Bar every Saturday night. When I'm driving home from bingo, I can always spot his truck. He tries to hide it on the side of the building. He thinks nobody sees it!"

"Oh, my Lord, and he goes to church on Sunday, as if he's holier than thou! Well, I must tell you about Jeb Howard. Did you know that he never puts more than a dollar in the offering plate? That old coot is rich. He don't trust banks neither. He keeps all his money hid inside his house."

"I heard that too! Rachel Simmon and me were just talkin' about that last week. Rachel knows for a fact that he keeps his money under his mattress. Old Jeb's not a millionaire, but he's darn close."

Several subscribers pick up their receivers to make a call every morning, but are unable to do so as long as Bernice and Penny are on the line. Some may snoop and listen until they are bored with their gossip. Others get impatient and demand that the two finish their talk so others can make a call. Sometimes there are shouting matches among the two ladies and other subscribers over phone time.

One person who wasn't really a snoop but just happened to pick up the receiver listened with keen interest about Jeb Howard's money. He waited until evening, just before dark, and drove his black Buick slowly past Jeb's house. He turned around at the nearest crossroad and passed by again. He saw there was no movement in the house, no vehicles in the driveway, and no lights were on inside the house. He decided that it would not be safe to park his car in the driveway, because Jeb may return home before he's finished inside. He saw no safe hiding spot nearby to park his car. He remembered an opening that was located by a graveled road, across a cornfield behind Jeb's house. He drove back to the opening and parked his car behind a small group of trees. He got out of his car and walked to the edge of the gravel to make sure that it was hidden from view of traffic. He remembered there was a child's Halloween mask on the backseat floor of his car. It was left there by the previous owner of the car he just purchased last month. He walked back to the car to retrieve the mask. It had the image of a sinister Mohawk Indian that would barely cover his face. It had only a thin rubber band strap to keep it on his head. *This will have to do.* When he felt comfortable enough about leaving the car there while he trekked across the cornfield to the rear of Jeb's house, he stopped near the edge of the cornfield and peeked through the stalks leaves to get a clear view. There no sign of anyone inside so far. There were no dogs growling or barking. The sun had descended past the trees in the horizon. He slowly walked closer and peeked through a window. The lights were off inside. He heard only silence. He tried turning the knob on the rear door, but it was locked. He thought about breaking the glass on the door but decided against it. He stooped down as he walked to the side of the house. He pushed upward on its window and it began to slide open. He continued pushing until it was wide enough to squeeze his large body frame through. He was in a bedroom. He turned his flashlight on and turned up the bed's top mattress to reveal the box spring, but no money was there. Next, he shined the light under the bed and found a small cardboard box. *Bingo!* He opened it, but it only contained a pair of pointed flat lady's shoes. Working quickly, he started rummaging through the closet, but after going through everything, he gave up and decided to venture into the hall area to another bedroom, if one existed. He reached the knob of a closed door, and it creaked just as he began to open it. His heart jumped when he heard a whisper coming from inside the room.

"I heard something, Jeb," Sally Howard whispered to her husband, Jeb.

Jeb had a string rigged to the bedpost. The opposite end of the string was tied to the light switch on the ceiling. He instantly pulled the string, turning on the ceiling light, before the intruder could back away. His mind was racing. He wasn't expecting them to be home. He wasn't considering that some farm families go to bed at dusk. Sally screamed. Jeb must have had an adrenaline rush because he jumped out of bed and grabbed his single shot twenty-gauge shotgun that was in the corner. The intruder rushed him, snatched the gun from his grip, and slammed his face with the butt of the gun.

"Where's the money!" the intruder shouted. Sally was still screaming. "Shut up! You won't get hurt if you tell me where the money is!"

Jeb was breathing heavily and blood was flowing from his broken nose. He pointed to his overalls lying over a chair. The intruder checked the pockets and fished out Jeb's wallet, but it contained only eight dollars.

"I know you have a lot of money hid. Where do you keep your stash?" the intruder asked again, as he put the barrel of the gun against Sally's forehead. "Tell me now!"

"Please, don't shoot her. All I have is in my wallet! It's all I have!" Jeb pleaded.

Sally was crying hysterically. "There ain't no money!"

The intruder poked Jeb hard in the ribs with the barrel of the shotgun and demanded both to get up. He pushed them, one at a time, out of the bedroom and ordered them to sit on the living room couch. Smoldering hot coal still burned in the fireplace. He grabbed the poker and stuck the tip into the hot coals. He pulled it out and placed it on Jeb's arm. Jeb howled in pain. He threw up his other arm in defense, and his hand flipped the intruder's mask upward, revealing his face.

"Tell me where you keep your stash, old man! I'm going to burn both of you until one of you tells me where the money is! You understand?"

"There is no money. Please believe me. There is no money. Don't burn him anymore!" Sally begged.

"You're lying! It's in this house somewhere! Tell me where it is!" He laid the hot poker on Sally's thigh, which singed her skin and emitted a sickening smell.

"We have no money, but we can get some. We don't have any here. Please, PLEASE! Don't burn us anymore!" pleaded Jeb.

The intruder was convinced they must be telling the truth. They wouldn't stand for this much pain without talking. The intruder just realized that the mask was no longer covering his face but was positioned askew on top of his head. They saw his face, and he couldn't allow them to live. In a rage, he smashed their heads repeatedly with the poker and ran out the front door with the Mohawk mask still positioned ridiculously crooked on top of his head.

*   *   *   *   *

A deputy sheriff was at our door notifying all the residents in the area about a double homicide nearby. An elderly couple, Jeb and Sally Howard, was robbed and brutally murdered by an unknown assailant.

"That's horrible! When did this happen?" asked Dad.

"What happened, Jake?" Mom asked as she came out of the kitchen and was startled to see a uniformed man at the door.

"They were discovered by their daughter, late this afternoon, when they didn't answer her calls yesterday," said the deputy. "The last time she spoke with her mother was Saturday afternoon. We think they were killed that night," the deputy responded.

"Any suspects?" Dad asked.

"No suspects yet. We are rounding up all the convicted felons in the area for questioning. We are doing all we can to find who did this, Mr. Johnson. I advise you to keep your doors locked and call the sheriff's department if any of you see anything suspicious."

"You're going back to work in the morning, Jake! We'll be alone all week," Mom said fearfully. "I'll be scared to death."

"Well, I have to go to work, Lily. It's my last week with the company. Then I'm home for good. Ya'll are gonna have to manage till then. Hopefully, this monster will be caught quickly."

The deputy would not reveal any details, but we got a few calls from frantic neighbors with gossip and rumors about the slayings. Violet called and said she heard that both were tortured with a hot poker and were beaten to death. It was unbelievable that such a heinous crime occurred so close to our own home. As the night wore on and the more tales we heard about the murders, it made us all jittery.

"George and Lisa are coming this weekend. Why don't you call and ask her if she can come earlier?" Dad asked.

"It's all over the news! We are watching it now!" Lisa announced when Mom called her about an early visit. "I can't believe that something that is horrible as this could happen anywhere, but it's so close to where you live! You must be terrified!"

"I have a big favor to ask you, Lisa," Mom said.

"What is it, sweetie?"

"Jake is going back to work tomorrow morning. We don't want to be alone out here in the country after what happened. Can ya'll come over tomorrow and stay with us?"

"You poor thing! Let me talk to George and I'll call you back, sweetie."

"Oh Lisa, it'll mean so much to us if you can do this. Call me collect."

"Don't be silly, Lily! I'm not calling my sister collect. You just hold on while I talk to George. Just sit tight. I'll call you in a few minutes."

"Is she out of her mind? I'm working until Friday," George said.

"I don't want Lily and the kids to be by themselves with a killer on the loose over there. That couple was tortured to death, and they lived only two miles away. You know there's been a lot of issues with Nancy too. I need to be there with them. I'll take a bus tomorrow and you can drive on down this weekend, George."

"Then you better call the bus station and make the arrangements."

*   *   *   *   *

"Great news, Lily! I just reserved a seat on Crossway Bus Lines and I'll be arriving tomorrow at 5 pm in Morris. George will be there Saturday. You'll pick me up?"

"Of course! We'll be there! We can't wait to see you."

"I'm so sorry about Nancy's problems. How is she doing now? She still having issues?"

"I'm worried to death about her. Jake took the day off so we could get her to the doctor. He says she is healthy, physically, but her nerves are shot. It was everything that's been happening. As I explained before, she had to leave her old school and her friends, and losing Zoomer was just too much for her. Too many things have happened, so close together, and she got to a breaking point. The doctor prescribed some medicine for her. I hope it helps. I'm at my wits' end."

"Do not fear, big sister. Aunt Lisa will be there tomorrow! Seriously though, I would like to spend some time with Nancy. Hopefully, I can help."

"I know you will, Lisa. You have always had a way with her. We are thrilled you are coming and I'm relieved."

"Is Levi okay?"

"Levi is fine. He loves it here. He seems to be adjusting well. Do you remember what I told you about our house? There is no running water and no indoor toilet."

"How can I forget that?"

Dad left for work the next morning, and it was the first day of the last week of his old job. His first stop was a meeting with his boss, Bob, who intended to make a plea for Dad to stay.

"How can you throw away fifteen years, Jake? We consider you as one of our very best. Besides, we are old friends. What can we do to make you stay?"

"I appreciate everything, Bob. As you know, we have relocated. I have another position that is waiting for me. I think I'm going to like it. I'll be home every night. My family needs me at home. I will be meeting Ralph, my replacement, at noon. He's a good man. He knows the business. He can handle the job."

"Ralph will not be meeting you. He decided not to take the promotion so you have no replacement. I'm asking you to, at least, stay on for another month. I'm sure your new employer will understand, Jake."

"Can't do it. I'll work this week, then I'm calling it quits."

"You know that you didn't give adequate notice. If you leave now and if things don't work out for you, then there may not be a place for you here if you ever want to come back. Think about that, Jake."

"I'm as sorry as I can be, but I'm moving on by the end of this week."

"Well, some friend you turned out to be!"

"Look, Bob, this has nothing to do with friendship. I've explained in detail about the new job offer, being away from home too much with Ace, and personal family matters." Dad stood up to leave.

"Screw you, Jake!"

"Screw you too, Bob!"

Dad finished the day, but was distracted by the exchange he had with his boss. His anger and frustration escalated by the hour. He started to drive back to the hotel that he usually stayed at, on that night but decided to go home for good instead. He had enough of Bob and the company after the excursion at the morning meeting. Besides, he was more nervous, than he led us to believe, about leaving us at home all week. *I'm going home. I'm not leaving my family alone while a homicidal maniac is on the prowl.* His mind was racing now. *Nancy's problem is getting far worse than I thought was possible. I need to be free this week to focus on her situation. It's too serious to ignore.* Dad turned the car around and drove home. Regardless of how his new position will work out, he destroyed any chance to return to the old one. While driving home that evening, he enjoyed a sense of freedom that he hadn't experienced in almost two decades.

At the same hour that Dad was "burning the bridges" with Bob, Nancy and I were just settling into our bus seats. Nancy was nervous about returning to school after her episodes over the weekend. She was worried about how her new friends from the party would react to her and especially Brad. He snubbed her at church and hadn't spoken to her since Friday night. Angie walked on the bus and politely sat with Nancy, as usual, but said little. Nancy sensed that Angie's mood wasn't the same, as well as the other girls who got on the bus at each stop. Before her first period session, Nancy was getting supplies from her locker when Johnny, one of Brad's friends who was at the sleepover, crept up behind her. He was aware of the witch episode at the party, as were every student at school, it seemed. As an intended harmless prank, he grabbed her arms from behind, and yelled "boo" loudly. Her endless screams spread through all reaches of the school building. She fell to the floor, her eyes rolled back, and she began to shake all over. Johnny claimed later at the principal's office that he was unaware of the emotional turmoil Nancy's plight at the party had caused her. Lily rushed to the school upon receiving a call about Nancy's "fainting spell," as it was described by the school secretary. Nancy went home sick for the rest of the day. Johnny received ten licks with a paddle that had holes drilled through the surface, to produce more sting to his buttocks. He also received fifty demerits and expelled for the day.

Aunt Lisa was busy doing the necessary preparation for her trip to our house. She still had to finish the laundry, pack her luggage, clean the house, and most importantly, prepare food to be refrigerated. Uncle George was helpless around the kitchen, according to Aunt Lisa, but she thought he could surely dump the stored dinners from the Tupperware storage containers to the appropriate pots and pans to heat again. She wished she had given him some pointers in stove operations. I've heard Aunt Lisa complain to Mom about his staunch aversion to women's work of any kind. During the weekdays, Aunt Lisa routinely watched her favorite soap operas such as *Guiding Light* and *General Hospital*. On that day, she was too busy getting ready for the trip and she had barely enough time to finish her work. However, she couldn't resist her addiction to her soaps and decided to turn the television on and listen to her shows as she worked. She was in the bedroom organizing her suitcase while straining to listen to the voice of Dr. Harding inform Nurse Brewer some distressful news. "We interrupt our regularly scheduled program to bring you a special report," the announcer said. Lisa rushed to the living room to watch. A familiar news reporter came on the air to make an announcement. "The residents of the sleepy town of Morris, Tennessee, are shaken by a double homicide of Jeb and Sally Howard, an elderly couple. They were found dead yesterday evening by a family member. The autopsy reports revealed the couple had been slain late Saturday night. The assailant is still at large, and the police have no suspects. It was reported that a witness had seen a man, who is believed to be over six feet in height, heavy built, and thought to be in his thirties, run through a field near the couple's home that same evening. Everyone is the area are advised to be cautious and report any suspicious activities to the local police department. Stay tuned for further developments."

Aunt Lisa reflected on the details about the murders that Mom had heard and talked about in their telephone conversations. She tried to grasp as to what kind of fiend would break into a home to torture and kill and for such evil to occur so close to where we lived. The thought made her want to stay in the safety of her own home, and she was tempted to find an excuse not to leave. Then she thought about the talk she had with Uncle George. "She's my sister," as she reasoned with George earlier. "She was terrified. I must go and be there for her," she had pleaded with George. Thinking about how much Mom needed her gave her courage to follow through on her promise to come.

"Didn't you take your medication this morning?" Mom asked Nancy after they arrived home.

"I just forgot," Nancy responded.

"Honey, it's so very important that you take the pills. I want you to handle this on your own, but I'm here if you need me." Mom wanted to make Nancy aware of the side effects but didn't want to make too much out of it for now. "If you feel dizzy or sad, then let me know. You will get used to the medication, all right, sweetie?" She decided to stop and say no more so not to seem like she was lecturing. She studied Nancy's blank expression. She had dark circles around her eyes and her hair was unkempt. "What could Nancy possibly be thinking?" Mom wondered.

Everything was racing through Nancy's mind. She dwelled on how her life was crumbling and she was helpless to stop it. The only thing that was going good for her was Brad. Now, he was gone. He no longer called and avoided her at school. He didn't even tell her why, but it really wasn't necessary. She already knew. Then an inner voice said to her sharply, "They're talking about you at school and telling lies. They're telling Brad lies. Lies, lies, LIES! Just ignore them. You don't need them."

Nancy's thoughts returned to the present to see Mom looking at her inquisitively. "What did you say?" she asked Mom.

"I said that you will get used to the medicine, sweetie. Please, try to remember to take your pills. It's important. Okay, honey?"

"I'll try."

CHAPTER SIX

AUNT LISA'S BUS arrived on time, and we were all there to meet her at the terminal. I was excited to see her, but Nancy balked. Mom wasn't about to leave her alone. Mom and Aunt Lisa had a jubilant reunion as I struggled to load the luggage into the trunk. On the way home, my aunt noticed how quiet and withdrawn Nancy was. She remembered how vivacious Nancy had always been in the past. She asked my sister about school, but she just mumbled a couple of inaudible words, barely above a whisper. My aunt and mom just looked at each other discerningly.

We passed a TV news truck from Nashville and then another one all the way from Atlanta. It was obvious that both were here because of the double murder. "There was a TV bulletin about the murders just before I left home," Aunt Lisa said in astonishment. "Is that why the news people are here?"

"Yeah, a deputy has been over. Cop cars have been going up and down our road too. That poor old couple only lived a couple of miles away," Mom said. "It has me scared to death."

"Have you heard anything about it? What did the deputy say?"

"He was the first to tell us about it. He was going around and asking everyone to report anything suspicious. We've been hearing all kinds of God-awful things that happened in that house. It's terrifying that something like this could happen so close. It has given me the willies."

I spoke up and said, "I heard they were tortured all night."

"That old couple were well known in this area," Mom said. "They had been living here all their lives. I heard they were just a nice quiet couple. They were tortured with a hot iron poker from the fireplace. Then they were beaten with it. I can't imagine anyone being so sadistic. The thought of someone like that still running loose terrifies me. Thank you, Lisa, for coming and staying with us."

"Do they have any suspects?" my aunt asked.

"No, but the area is crawling with cops."

We got home just before dark, and Lisa was shocked at the run-down condition of our farmhouse but didn't comment about it in front of Nancy and me. Her first order of business was to visit the "outside bathroom," as she called it. I laughed at the name she had for our outhouse.

"Follow me," Mom responded, as she led Aunt Lisa out the back door.

As soon as they stepped outside, Aunt Lisa instantly saw the outhouse and could not contain her disbelief. "This is it? Oh Lily, why in the world did you let Jake buy a place like this?"

Mom laughed nervously but inwardly was embarrassed. The remark made her feel ashamed. "Lisa, we been through this. I thought you understood."

My aunt could read Mom's feelings. "I'm sorry, Lily. I shouldn't have said it like that. I know you told me. You described everything. I know you got a great deal on the place, and Jake wanted a farm for so long. It's just I thought you were exaggerating. I had a different image in my mind." She realized that she was saying all the wrong things. She came here to help at a time when we were in need, and things were getting off to a bad start. "It can be made beautiful!" She was trying to limit her insensitive comments now. "Of course, you just moved here, and ya'll haven't had time to do a lot of improvements yet. The scenery is so beautiful! I see a lot of promise in this place."

Nancy was peering through the window at Mom and Aunt Lisa as they were having, what she thought, was a discussion about her, no doubt. *They must be talking shit about you, Nancy,* the voice inside her said. *What other reason would they sneak outside to talk? They could have had their little talk in here, just as easily, but no, they had to go outside so you couldn't hear them talk trash about you, Nancy. Why do you think your stupid aunt came here to begin with? They are all plotting against you.* Nancy stormed off to her room when Mom and Aunt Lisa began walking back to the house.

"Where did Nancy go?" Aunt Lisa asked.

"In her room," Mom was talking in a low voice so Nancy could not hear. "That's where she stays most of the time. We took her to the doctor and he prescribed a sedative for her," replied Mom.

"Oh my. Is the sedative helping?"

"We got the prescription filled yesterday and we had her to take one. By the afternoon, she went outside to sit on the front porch and she was talking to the neighbors who were walking by. Her appetite had improved last night and she was actually sociable during supper. So I guess you could say that the pills are helping. She has been so withdrawn." Mom was still speaking in a silenced tone, so not to be overheard by Nancy.

"What about her fainting spells that you told me about, over the phone?" Aunt Lisa asked.

"She fainted today at school. I had to bring her home early. We'll talk about that later when we have more privacy," Mom whispered and placed her forefinger, vertically, to her lips as the telephone rang.

"Hello?" Mom asked when she picked up the receiver.

"It's me. I'm on my way home," Dad said.

"Are you serious? You're really coming home, Jake? What happened?"

"Yeah, that meeting with Bob didn't go well this morning. The man I was training to replace me changed his mind. He wants to stay with the route that he has. So Bob tried to talk me in to staying, at least for a month. When I wouldn't do it, he turned against me. We almost came to blows. I'm calling it quits. I'm coming home."

"You're not gonna finish the week?"

"The men can handle things on their own until they get a new manager. I have too much to do before starting with the utility company next week."

"What if the new company doesn't work out?"

"It'll have to work out because I'm not going back. Is Lisa there yet?"

"Yeah, she's here and she's getting settled in."

"Great! Be sure and tell her that she better be prepared for some good old country hospitality! How does she like the place?"

"Wait and I'll ask her. Jake wants to know how you like the farm so far, Lisa?"

"Tell him that I love his outhouse!" Lisa laughed before she realized she may have just made a bad joke.

Mom laughed and said, "Lisa said that she loves . . ."

Dad stopped her before she could finish and said, "I heard her." They both were laughing.

"So when can we expect you, Jake?"

"I'm working my way there. It should be in two to three hours. Don't wait up."

"We'll only sleep so well with a crazy guy on the loose. Thank goodness Lisa is here, and you will be home tonight! Praise God! I must tell you about what happened to Nancy. A boy sneaked up behind her, at school, and scared her so bad she passed out. I went up there to get her and brought her home. The boy got a good paddling and was sent home."

"Oh my God, Lily! How is she now?"

Mom looked toward Nancy's room to make sure her door was closed. "I can't talk too loud, Jake. Nancy is in her room and her door is closed, but I'm afraid she may hear me. She didn't take her pill this morning. I talked to her when we got home. I'll just tell you more when you get here."

"That's another reason I'm coming home. This is too serious to work another few days if I don't absolutely have too and I don't. Especially after what happened at that damn meeting this morning with Boob, I mean Bob."

"You meant 'Boob,' Jake. That's not nice. Stop talking silly and come on home."

"I know Lisa is there with you and the kids, but I've been thinking and I'll feel better if I was there. I don't want any of you to be alone, at home, all night."

"There's been news people in the area today from Nashville, and Atlanta too. There's been police and sheriff cars in the area. I feel better already that Lisa is here, but I can't wait for you to get here. Please drive carefully, honey."

"Don't worry. I'll keep it between the ditches. See ya'll when I get there. Bye."

"This is Jake's last day at his job. He got in a fight with Bob, his boss, and decided not to finish out his notice. I hope that's not a mistake," Mom said to Lisa.

"I heard ya'll talking. I'm sure Jake knows what he's doing. He's a smart man. Don't worry, Lily. Jake is starting his new job soon? Next week, you said before?"

"Next Monday. I'm happy about that. He's really excited about it. I just wish he wouldn't just up and leave his old job, like he did."

"It sounds impressive. You said that he'll be home every night? It'll be nice having him home after all these years. George is happy for you too. He's looking forward to this weekend when he gets here."

I turned on the television and a news station was reporting the double murders.

The local sheriff's department and statewide law enforcement were hushed about much of the details. The police discreetly interviewed residents to gather facts before informing the public. However, rumors were flying, thanks to the county's party line system. One such rumor was that the police have a suspect.

The autopsies were finally completed and revealed to the public. Nashville's Action News had the official report. In a TV bulletin, the news station reported that both died from being bludgeoned, in the head, with a fireplace poker. Both had suffered from severe beatings to their head and bodies. There are no suspects yet in custody.

"Well, it seems the rumors, for the most part, have been confirmed," Lisa said.

"Let's turn the TV off. I can't believe they would be that graphic," Mom said in disgust.

"I agree, but I think nothing this awful rarely happens."

"Mom, what does 'bludgeon' mean?" I asked.

"Levi! It means getting hit hard with an object. Now, turn the television off or change the channel."

"I can't imagine anyone being that evil. Oh, the nightmare those two went through gives me chills," Mom told Lisa. "I once read in a true-crime magazine that sick people like this don't stop. They keeping killing until caught. Nobody will rest while this fiend is on the loose."

"To think it was a nightmare is an understatement, but I know what you mean. I'm glad that Jake will get back tonight too. I'm curious, do ya'll have a gun?"

"Jake has a shotgun. Levi has a rifle that we bought for him last Christmas."

"Don't worry, I'll shoot him!" I bragged.

"I know you will, sweetie. Levi is such a darling," said Lisa. "Well, you can have more target practice out here, than in the city! What kind of rifle is it?"

"It's a .22. I shoot birds, mostly," I said.

"Stop shooting those little birds, Levi!" Mom said sternly. "He shot a mockingbird yesterday. That's the state bird. That's illegal. We could be fined for that," said Mom. "You do that again and your dad will take the gun away!"

"Yes, ma'm," I replied.

"You gonna let me ride your horse tomorrow, aren't you, Levi?" asked Lisa.

"Sure! His name is Sam. He's really easy to ride."

"I look forward to riding him. I'm sorry about your dog, by the way."

Aunt Lisa's mention of Zoomer brought back horrible memories. It wasn't the thought of him getting killed that haunted me as much as Nancy's breakdown. She scared the hell out of me the way she was shaking and in an apparent trance.

"We buried Zoomer in the backyard," I responded.

"Perhaps you can get another one. You certainly have plenty of room for one."

"We plan to when Nancy is ready. Jake plans to buy some chickens and cows. All I want is a bathroom and kitchen sink."

"No doubt ya'll will get this farm shaping up soon enough! I'm so proud of your courage to buy it."

"It's taking its toll us, especially Nancy."

"Oh, the poor thing. I'm sure she'll adjust to everything eventually and get through her problems."

Mom leaned over to Aunt Lisa, put her arms around her, and began to sob.

CHAPTER SEVEN

IT WAS FALL harvest in Morris and farmer Billy Allen was pulling his second-hand corn harvester, which he just bought, toward his five-acre field, two miles away from his home. He had been growing corn on this track for the last seven years. This was the first year that he would not have to harvest each individual ear of corn by hand with the help of his wife and daughter. He was so excited about using his harvester that he hardly slept the previous night. The machine was moving slowly behind his aging tractor, and it took up the narrow road as a string of commuters trailed behind, unable to pass. Some of the drivers were impatiently blowing their horns and shouting for Billy to move to the side so they could pass. He loved the attention. Three cars back, from the harvester, was a patrol car driven by Sheriff James Diller, accompanied by Senior Deputy Joe Wilson.

"You want me to hit the siren, Sheriff?" Deputy Wilson asked.

"Relax, this is not an emergency. The state boys are already there. It's not much farther."

The officers were driving to the area that Mary Weaver claimed she saw someone exiting a cornfield around 2:00 a.m. It was at the same estimated time frame when the double homicide took place. Mrs. Weaver was awakened when her dog started barking. "Tootsie don't ever bark like that at that time of night. She sleeps with me ever since Fred, God rest his soul, died three years ago. If Tootsie has to go outside to do her business, then she just gets in my face and whines. I just let her out before I went to bed, about eleven, and I know she didn't have to go again so soon. I never let her do her business in the house. I always make her go outside in the front yard. She was in the living room and just barking up a storm. I peeked through the blinds, and I saw a man walking out of the cornfield down at the corner's crossing. I saw him clear as day. The moon was bright that night. I can sure say, without doubt, that the man was as big as one of those wrestlers I see on TV, and he was tall! I don't scare easily because I have Fred's twelve-gauge, and I keep it loaded, but seeing that guy sneaking around at that time of night scared me to death."

The sheriff and other state law enforcement were suspicious because Howard's land started on the other side of the cornfield.

When Billy approached his cornfield, he was surprised to see two black cars blocking the gate entrance. He stopped his tractor and climbed off. "Who are you and what in hell are you doing?" Billy demanded.

"We are state detectives and this area is off limits," Detective John Snider responded. "We will be searching this area for evidence in the Howard murder case. We will be sealing the area off until further notice. Are you Mr. Allen?"

"Hell, yeah! This is my land and I need to get in there and harvest my corn! Why didn't somebody let me know?"

"Discretion is protocol during an investigation prior to and during the process of collecting physical evidence, sir. Your personal property could be subject to confiscation from this area. You'll be issued a receipt for each item, and they will be returned to you as soon as soon possible. The scene must be untouched so you cannot enter until the search is complete."

The traffic was stalled behind the harvester so Sheriff Diller flipped on the blue light and zapped the siren for the cars in front to move to the side so he could pass. He and Deputy Wilson exited the patrol car and asked Billy to move his tractor and to the side of the road so the other vehicles could pass. After some resistance, Billy complied.

"Mr. Allen, I would like for you to come with us to the sheriff's office for questioning. You can leave your tractor and machinery here. Someone will bring you back here after the questioning," the sheriff said.

"What the hell for?" Billy responded. "I ain't done nothing! I didn't kill those people!"

"We are questioning everyone in the area, sir." That part was right for the sheriff was questioning everyone who lived in the area. Billy certainly fit the description as Mrs. Weaver detailed. He stood, at least, six feet tall and he had a big frame, as lots of men. Billy owned the property where Mrs. Weaver saw the possible suspect. It was not much to go on but was worth following up on. Sheriff Diller decided to run a background check anyway, and bingo—Billy was court-martialed in the army for sexual violence. He received a dishonorable discharge and served four years in the United States Penitentiary, Leavenworth.

"Is there anything you would like to tell me?" Sheriff Diller asked Billy while he sat in small back room in the sheriff's headquarters.

"I already told you that I didn't kill nobody."

"Is there anything else you would like to tell me?" Diller was watching Billy's body movement.

"Huh, if you are talking about my time in prison, that was a long time ago. I did my time."

"Where were you last weekend?"

"I was at home with my wife. Listen, I told you I didn't kill those people. I've never killed anybody. I've stayed out of trouble after I got out of prison. I never want to go to prison again. I learnt my lesson. I've worked hard to make a better life."

"Your wife will vouch for you that you were home each night, Saturday and Sunday?"

"Please don't get my wife involved in this!"

"Were you in the same cornfield that we met you at earlier today, over the weekend, day or night, Billy?"

"I wasn't, I swear, but why do you want to know?"

"A witness saw somebody about your size in that cornfield, early Sunday morning."

Billy was almost in tears. "It wasn't me, I swear. I was at home with Molly."

"Don't leave town, Billy. You stay close to home. You hear me?"

Billy was blubbering. "Yes, sir. Can I go now?"

"What do ya' think, boss?" Deputy Wilson asked after Billy exited the building.

"He's either a clever liar or he's not our man," answered Diller.

*   *   *   *   *

While Billy was being questioned, state detectives were at his home with a search warrant and to question Billy's wife, Molly. She was confused when approached by the detectives at the front door, then she was mad. "Ya'll want to ask me questions? What in hell is this about?" she demanded.

"We are investigating the murder of Jeb and Sally Howard," Detective Paul Summers responded as his partner, Detective Frank Booker, began a visual search of the room. "Where was your husband Saturday and Sunday?"

"I don't have to tell you shit! He was doing his work. How in the hell should I know! I can't keep up with the sombitch every minute of the day! You think Billy killed those people? You're really full of it, you know that?"

"Mrs. Allen, a heinous crime has been committed. I'm asking you to cooperate with the investigation. If we can clear your husband, then we can move on. Was your husband doing his work at night?"

"No, he don't do his farm work at night. He's always here at night, stupid."

"He's at home every night. He didn't leave the house over the weekend at night?"

"I told you he was here!" Molly looked around at the other detective rummaging in her closet. "What in hell are you doing!"

"We have a search warrant," responded Detective Booker, "as Detective Summers informed you." Booker was filling a bag with three pairs of shoes he found in the closet.

"Why are you taking his shoes?" Molly asked.

"We will give you a receipt of any property we confiscate, and they will be returned when the investigation is resolved. Relax, ma'am," Booker warned.

The detectives took Billy's shoes, for outsole impressions. Footprints found in the cornfield or on the bloodstained floor of the murder scene was to be compared. If they are a match, then forensic experts were to return for a full analysis, including dusting for fingerprints.

"I almost feel sorry for poor Billy when he has to face that old battle axe that he's married to," Detective Booker joked as he drove away. He and Detective Summer were still laughing when they got back to the precinct.

*   *   *   *   *

His inner thoughts were screaming. The carnage he created and the trouble he made for himself set his nerves in overdrive. *What was I thinking? I really botched things up. No one was supposed to die. It was supposed to be easy. It was a sure thing. Break in, get the cash, and get out and my money problem would have been behind me. I found someone that I really love. Someone who cares about me, who I found a way to keep loyal and not leave me. I must find another way. I must get my precious away from this hick town, with these narrow-minded hicks. I'm sick of their jokes, their sneers, and their laughs. We don't belong here. We need to go far away, especially now. The whole area is crawling with cops. No one knows it was me. Nobody suspects me. I must stay low and be patient.*

CHAPTER EIGHT

"WHY DON'T YOU make that lazy son of yours get a job!" exclaimed Everett. "I'm getting tired of him laying around all day, smoking cigarettes! How can he afford to smoke?"

"That poor boy been sick. He's not able to do a lot," replied Violet.

"Bull! He's not sick. He's just too sorry to work. He's worthless as a tit on a boar. You spoil him sick, Violet. He's a grown man. I'm getting him a job at the nursery. We'll work that sickness out of 'em. If he wants to keep living here, he's gonna pay his way. It'll teach him some responsibility."

"He can't do that kind of work! He has a bad back! Don't you bother him about working there. He's gonna do something better with his life than work at that farm you work at."

"Violet, he quit school in the tenth grade. He's just lazy and useless. He's always gonna be useless as long has you mother him. If he don't go get a job, then maybe he ought to move out."

"Move out? He can't! It would kill me." Violet was crying and pleading with Everett not to make Larry leave. "He's got no money. He's got no place to go."

"Why don't he move in with that queer?"

"Who? Who are you talking about, Everett?"

"You know who I'm talking about, old woman. That darn Jerry."

"He ain't!"

"Yeah, he is. So is Larry. You don't think I know about that sissy boy of yours? You don't think I know what's going on with those two?"

"My boy is not that way! Don't you say that about Larry! He's a good Christian boy! You leave him alone. He's not moving out. You can't make him. There's nuthin' wrong with him. Jerry is his daddy. That's all!"

"Daddy? You signed papers so that he could adopt Larry when he was sixteen years old. He was almost grown then. You didn't even tell me about it. That boy turned seventeen, just after that."

"Jerry loves Larry as a son. Jerry is good to him and takes care of him. Larry never had a daddy. His real daddy ran off. He never cared anything about me or Larry. You never was a daddy to him either."

"I just never spoiled him like you. I gave him chores and made him do 'em. I don't want Jerry in this house. Ya' hear me, woman? I know about them sleeping in the same bed last week. I'll have none of that vile sin in this house. It's just plain sin! I don't want Tommy being around that kind of doings."

"We don't got nowhere else for Jerry to sleep. You got a dirty mind, old man. Larry is a good boy. Jerry prayed with us last Sunday."

"He'll sleep at his own place and he can take that boy of yours with him. Do you think our good neighbors don't know what's going on? You don't know a darn thing about that Jerry feller. He said he's from Memphis, but he don't sound like he's from there."

*   *   *   *   *

You would think that Dad was gone for a year, instead of just a day, the way my mom embraced him when he walked through the door. Lisa was relieved too, considering Nancy's issues and a heinous murderer on the loose.

Dad was really starting to be worried about Nancy's mental stability but waited until he and Mom had privacy, in their bedroom, to discuss it. "I've been thinking while on my drive home, honey. I've underestimated Nancy's behavior. I thought it would pass."

"What are we going to do, Jake? Nancy is a wreck. We must help her through this. I'm not even sure she's stable enough to go to school in the morning."

"I think we should make sure she goes. Sitting in her room and moping all day isn't going to help her. When she gets home, we'll show her how much we love her. Hopefully, she'll open up to us and tell us what she's feeling."

It was after midnight, and my parents were finally going to go to bed. Nancy was in her room all evening. Mom peeked in and was more at ease to see that she was asleep. "Nancy will need her rest tonight. After her episode at school today, she will have to face the other students tomorrow," Mom told Dad when she returned to their bedroom. They decided earlier that they would drive Nancy and me to school the next day. Afterward, they planned to visit the school counselor to discuss Nancy's plight.

"We are glad you came in, Mr. and Mrs. Johnson," Herman Smith, the principal of Morris High School, said cheerfully. "Welcome to our community. I am certain that Nancy will have a pleasurable learning experience at our school."

"Thank you. We are here to see the school counselor, but I want to speak with you too," Dad said.

"I understand."

"We are concerned about the incident that occurred yesterday. Relocating has been traumatic for Nancy, and we don't appreciate any of the kids sneaking up and scaring her. Am I clear on this, Mr. Smith?"

"Absolutely, Mr. Johnson. The student involved yesterday was sternly disciplined. I can assure you that our teachers are highly trained to deal with such incidences. Please have a seat while I call Mr. Henson, our school counselor."

"We are very sorry about what happened yesterday," Mr. Henson said to my parents at a closed-door meeting.

"That's what we would like to discuss with you, Mr. Henson," Dad said. "As we just informed Mr. Smith, we cannot tolerate any student mistreating Nancy. She's having trouble adjusting since we moved here. It's vital that the staff be on guard for her welfare."

"Yes, sir. May I ask if there had been any drastic changes in Nancy's moods recently?"

"Yeah, that's why we insist that you be on guard for our daughter's welfare," Mom said.

"We have spoken to some of the students who witnessed yesterday's unfortunate incident. They all tell us the same account of what happened. They say that the student involved is certainly guilty of frightening your child. However, none of the kids seems to feel that it was not enough to cause such an extreme reaction from her . . ."

"Just what do you mean by that!" Dad asked angrily before Mr. Henson could finish.

"I say this out of the highest respect for your daughter and for you. From what we know, based on the accounts of the other students that saw what happened, she fell to the floor on her back. Her eyes were literally rolled back, and only the whites of her eyes were visible, Mr. and Mrs. Johnson. She was shaking all over. She was very disoriented afterward."

"Oh, my Lord," Mom said uneasily.

"My job is to help with the students' academic achievements. Although it's early in the school year, Nancy has not completed any of her schoolwork. I see in her records at her previous school that she was a straight A student," the counselor added.

"Thank you for your time," Dad concluded.

* * * * *

In Nancy's mind, every student was gawking as she made her way down the hall to her locker. She could hear the whispers, or at least she imagined. "Hi, Nancy! Feeling better?" a student asked, but what was the student's name? Nancy couldn't recall. She ignored her classmates as she walked to class. The pill that Mom had her swallow, just before exiting the car earlier, put her in a trancelike state through her first-class session. As she walked to her second class, she noticed her parents exiting the administrator's office at the other end of the hall. As the day went by and as the prescribed medicine for her nerves wore off, she thought more and more about her parents' visit to school. Her mind was racing. At lunch period, she was sitting in an empty classroom with the lights out. Paranoia was taking over her mind.

Miss Pruitt, the algebra teacher at Morris High School, was walking through the same hallway, as she had every school day, for the past forty years. Moving with a limp, due to arthritis, she frequently reminisced about her favorite students through the years and their whereabouts today. "They are probably living full lives with careers and married with children, I'm sure," she thought to herself. She reflected about her own life and how she never married. She stopped when she approached room 203. She stared at the numbers over the door for a moment, and old memories began racing through her mind. She was fighting back tears as she remembered the first year, in 1925, that she taught in this very same room. Mark Summers, assistant coach, and the heartthrob among teachers at Morris High stopped in the hallway and smiled at her. She returned the smile as she stood behind the podium. They soon started dating, and Miss Pruitt found the love of her life. Both of them were filled with promise and excitement for the future. She remembered wearing flapper-style dresses to go dancing with Mark on Saturday nights. They would do dances such as the Charleston and foxtrot. She remembered their first kiss while they did the waltz. They began seeing each other daily and their love blossomed.

One morning during a class period, Mark became unusually tired. He thought about going home for the day but knew his students would be without a teacher for the remaining day. However, he didn't report to school the next day because of a fever. Ultimately, he was examined by a doctor who admitted

Mark into the local hospital. After only three weeks, he died of leukemia. "That was long ago, but it seemed like just yesterday," Miss Pruitt recollected as she stared at the numbers, "203," over the door. "Broken dreams from long ago," she reflected as she tried to regain her composure.

Her train of thought was disrupted when suddenly she was startled by a movement that was visible through the glass-paned door of the darkened room. She opened the door and entered to investigate. "Who's in there?" she asked.

Nancy panicked and raced toward the exit. She collided with Miss Pruitt, who fell backward and hit the floor, hard, but Nancy keep running. *How did they find me? How did they know I was in that room?* She hurried out of a side door just when Mr. Neal, a geometry teacher, was coming in and he stopped her.

"Where you going so fast? The second bell has rung. You trying to sneak out?" Mr. Neal asked but Nancy didn't answer. "Which class should you be in?"

Nancy returned to reality and struggled to answer. "Social studies," she whispered.

"You're late for your social studies class. If I find you trying to skip class again, you'll be going to the principal's office. You understand me?"

"Yeah."

"What was that you said?"

"Yes, sir."

"What's your name?"

"Nancy, sir."

"Well, Nancy, you better get going."

Moments later, the bell rang, signaling the end of the class period. Dozens of students were hurrying out of the other classrooms to find Miss Pruitt lying on the floor in the doorway of room 203. Several kids were huddling around her, while others stood in utter shock. Finally, other teachers were running to her aid. An emergency call was made to the telephone operator, who called an ambulance and the police.

Miss Pruitt regained consciousness in the Morris General Hospital. She had cracked her skull and broke a femur from the fall. The doctor and police quizzed her about the events that led up to the incident. She had no memory of what happened. No physical ailment was found that may have caused the fall. It was assumed that she just tripped and fell. She was bedridden for months. She was totally dependent on the orderlies, who rolled her over daily, to prevent bed sores and infection. They assisted her with a bedpan for urination and defecation. She eventually slipped into dementia and died alone in her bed, four months after her fall.

CHAPTER NINE

U NCLE GEORGE ROLLED in the following Saturday, following Aunt Lisa's Tuesday arrival. He was also unimpressed by our decision to buy a farm, or at least this one. They were both glad to be leaving early Monday morning, I suspected. The hardship of using the outhouse and no indoor water for a bath, even for a few days, was more than they could stand. Likewise, Dad was relieved to see them go. On that same Monday morning, Dad started his new job, which allowed him to be home each evening. Such freedom gave him ample time for home projects.

Three months after we moved to the farm, we finally had an indoor bathroom and a kitchen sink built. Our next project was buying a milk cow. Dad milked it and carried the off-white, almost yellow-like milk into the house. Nancy and I stood over the milk pail lying on the kitchen table in disgust. Dad tried to explain that the color was harmless, and it would still taste like milk. "The color is just from the flowers in the pasture that the cow has been eating," Dad claimed. We weren't convinced. Only Mom and Dad would drink it. Eventually, she started using store-bought milk again, which was commercially generated through a processing plant before it was packaged and shipped to the markets.

We visited a chicken farm and bought a dozen hens, for their eggs, and a rooster. Nancy and I wouldn't eat their eggs. We built a chicken pen, but some of the hens actually flew over it. Two of them had wandered into the road and were ran over by drivers passing by. Dad's new boss, Ron, had a teenage son who raised a beautiful white rooster inside his home. It was an Easter gift when it was a baby chick. They lived in town, and the Easter rooster outgrew its surroundings, so we agreed to adopt it. Apparently, it wasn't a good idea because within a week, the rooster disappeared without a trace. We speculated that since it was raised indoors, it was unaware of the dangers of living outside. A hawk may have swooped down and carried it away. With the help of Everett, we decided to slaughter the remaining chickens to eat, since they were too much trouble to maintain. I shot some through the brain, with my .22 rifle. Dad ran down the rest and ringed their necks. Everett plucked and cleaned them.

Everett and Violet proved to be very good-hearted neighbors. We moved to our farm too late for the planting season to plant a garden. The Reeves had a surplus of cucumbers and tomatoes from their own garden. Violet insisted we take several bushels of these vegetables for canning. Mom admitted that she didn't know anything about the art of canning vegetables, so Violet walked her through the entire process. They jokingly made a deal. Violet would teach Mom country ways, and Mom agreed to teach her city ways.

*   *   *   *   *

Nancy continued to struggle with school grades by spring. Dad decided to visit our school, during his lunch hour, and called Mom, who was at home, to meet him there. The guidance counselor informed my parents that she was in danger of failing the ninth grade.

"The only resolve would be a remarkable pickup in grades," Mr. Henson warned.

"We'll look for a tutor," Mom said in desperation, to spare Nancy the humiliation of repeating a grade.

"Your daughter seems to have no interest in learning. She continues to not do her homework. She's been skipping classes and failing tests. As we discussed last fall, based on Nancy's academic record, she's highly intelligent and can do the work, but she's not trying."

"Oh Jake, we cannot let her fail!" Mom pleaded.

Later, while they were in the school parking lot, Dad said that he would get professional counseling for Nancy. "We will have a sit-down talk with Nancy tonight. I have to get back to work."

"The medicine, at least, prevents her from having those spells," Mom added.

After she left school, Mom ran some errands and still hadn't returned home when Nancy and I stepped off the bus. I immediately ran to the barn to saddle Sam for a ride. Nancy walked inside the house and straight to her room as usual. Being alone in the house was rare. Nancy was standing before her dresser mirror and pondering the change of events that has shaken her life to its core. She thought about Brad, who she was very close to, but who then totally ignored her. She thought about her friends, who avoided her. She thought about her inability to concentrate in class and her failing grades. She looked deeply at her reflection. *Who have I become?*

That evening after supper, Dad told me to leave the room. Before Nancy had a chance to get up from the kitchen table, Dad asked her about her grades. "Your mom and I had a talk with the guidance counselor today, Nancy. It seems you have no interest in your studies. You are going to fail the ninth grade. You will have to repeat the whole year. Do you realize that?"

"My grades are not that bad."

"Nancy, yes, they are! Are you listening? The only way for you to pass is to make straight As. That's the only way you will pass. You have been missing your assignments, skipping classes, and failing tests. You will have to make a complete turnaround between now and the end of the school year."

"I'll do better," Nancy said with an almost inaudible whisper.

"You'll need to put a mental effort required to learn the material at school and at home. Do not skip any more classes. Do you understand?"

Tears ran down her cheeks, and she began to rock back and forth. "O-o-o-okay," Nancy stuttered.

"Your mother and I know you have the aptitude, Nancy. You've been an honor student until this year. You have completely stopped applying yourself. We have decided to arrange for you to be tutored. On Tuesdays and Thursdays, you will report to Mrs. Foutch. She is also a counselor. We also meet her today. She can help with whatever is troubling you. Okay, Nancy?"

"For how l-l-l-long?"

"Two hours each day until the last week of school this year. Don't be late or skip any of these sessions. Mrs. Foutch will report to me immediately if you are. Are you hearing me, Nancy?"

"Y-y-y-yeah."

"I suggest you don't waste any time. You better get started on tomorrow's assignments."

Nancy stood in front on her dresser mirror again that night, after midnight. An inner voice spoke. *Nancy? Close your eyes, Nancy. Turn slowly. I believe in the bell witch. Say it, Nancy.* She did as the voice commanded. *Do it again, Nancy. Turn slowly and say, I believe in the bell witch. Say it, Nancy.* She did again as the voice commanded. *One more time, Nancy. Turn! Turn, Nancy! Say it again! I believe in the bell witch! Say it, Nancy! Say it!* Nancy repeated it one more time. *Open your eyes, Nancy. Open them!* Nancy resisted. *Open your eyes, Nancy!*

Nancy was unable to look away from the cold, blood red eyes. Its skin, covered with boils, were repulsive and even stank of decay. It extended its gaunt hand that passed through the mirror. *Take my hand, Nancy.* It was if two voices were speaking in unison as before at the slumber party. *Take my hand, Nancy, and come with me.* Nancy's level of terror was incomprehensible. *Take my hand and come with me, Nancy!* She lifted her arm slowly. Her hand only inches from the clutches of the bell witch. Its hand thrust forward and clinched Nancy's. She felt her body elevating. She was floating. The bell witch possessed total dominance over Nancy.

Nancy slowly walked out of her bedroom with her hand held out in front of her, as if being led by an invisible force. She walked through the kitchen to the back door and stopped. She extended her other hand and opened the door and stepped out.

Mom knocked on Nancy's and my bedroom door to awaken us for school. Then she headed to the kitchen and noticed the back door was open. She distinctly remembered locking the back door, along with the front one, the night before. She had always made it point to be a nightly routine, especially since the double murders last fall.

"No, I didn't open it last night," Dad responded when Mom asked.

Dad came into my room while I was getting up. "Did you go outside last night, Levi?"

"No. I was sleeping all night," I responded.

Dad walked into Nancy's room and saw that she wasn't there. "Nancy, where are you?" he shouted as he walked through the house. "Lily, where is Nancy?"

"She's not in her room?" Mom asked, worriedly.

"She's not in the house." Dad walked out into the backyard, in his boxer shorts, but no Nancy.

"Oh my God, Jake! Where could she be?"

"I don't know, Lily!" Dad started shouting for Nancy. He walked around to the front section of the house to check on the cars. There was a remote possibility that Nancy could have gone joyriding with friends. He didn't think that she would take one of the cars on her own, since Nancy did not how to drive, to his knowledge.

"Levi, go see if your sister is in the barn!" Dad shouted as he scrambled to put on his shirt and pants.

"I didn't see her. She's not in the barn," I reported when I returned.

"I'll drive around the area. With her mind, she could be wandering around in the road."

"Jake, don't say that," Mom said.

"Well, Lily, if you have a better plan, then let's hear it!" Dad said angrily.

"Oh, Jake, I'll stay here in case she comes back," Mom reasoned.

Dad drove up one side of the road and down the other. He stopped to ask Everett, who was in his yard, if he'd seen Nancy. Everett said that he had not seen her, but after Dad continued driving on his search, he had got on the party line to ask some neighbors if they had seen Nancy. The party line eavesdroppers called their friends and neighbors in the area to be on the lookout for Nancy. Some of the neighbors started search parties. After an hour with no sight of Nancy, Dad called Sheriff Diller and asked if we could file a missing person report immediately, but officially, the sheriff's department cannot file a report until twenty-four hours after Nancy is missing.

"Mr. Johnson, is it possible that she sneaked out, in the night, to party with friends or is with a boyfriend?"

"I know my daughter, Sheriff. Besides, even if she left with friends, she wouldn't leave the door open. She's been keeping to herself lately. She hasn't been socializing with any of the other kids. She hasn't had a boyfriend in months."

My parents and the sheriff went through a slew of question on a missing-persons checklist, including the places Nancy frequented, recreational activities, drug use, and garments she was wearing.

"Does your daughter have any mental health issue that I should know about?" Since we lived in a small community where the party line was a major source of social networking, in that day, Sheriff Diller was aware of rumors about Nancy. Besides, Dad said that Nancy hadn't been mingling with other kids.

Mom winced and hesitated, but for the sake of helping Nancy to be found quicker, acknowledged that she had been distant and antisocial. The sheriff radioed in the information to the dispatcher, who relayed it to all of the deputies and search parties.

Within an hour after receiving my parents' missing-person's report, the sheriff's department received a call from Ethel Judd, reporting that her husband, Clyde, didn't come home last night.

CHAPTER TEN

C LYDE JUDD, A weekend regular at
the Blue Mule, was dreading the drive
home and facing his wife, Ethel. He knew she would be waiting up. He normally
didn't go to the Mule on weekdays, but he got a good price on the cows he
hauled to the stockyard earlier and that's a good enough reason to celebrate
as any. Not that he needed an excuse to take a drink. He had plenty stashed
in the barn that he could have anytime. Ethel didn't allow him to keep it in
the house. Alvin, the bartender, who had announced closing time, was giving
Clyde the eye to leave.

"Mix me a good 'un for the road," Clyde pleaded with Alvin. Clyde reached
in his wallet and pulled out a large stack of one-hundred-dollar bills, struggling
to find a single one-dollar one.

"Can't do it, Clyde. Careful carrying that much cash. Go on home now.
Your old lady's gonna kick your ass as it is. Don't make it any worse." Alvin
had been keeping a watch on a stranger sitting at the end of the bar who had
been eyeing Clyde's wallet whenever he opened it to buy another beer. The
man was conspicuous looking because of his large size, but he left the bar a
little earlier.

Clyde slid off the barstool and was slightly off balanced but regained his
composure. While he headed for the exit, Alvin warned him of Deputy Sheriff
Duke, who patrolled the area on the night shift. Clyde nervously sat in his
pickup truck and rummaged through the glove box, hoping to find a stick of
gum to help conceal his whiskey breath. He looked at his watch. *Shit! It's 2:15.*

Ethel will be on the warpath! He started the truck and looked in every direction for patrol cars staked out. He put the shift in first gear and realized he should have used the bathroom before leaving the bar. He decided to take the back roads on the five-mile drive. Clyde Judd never made it home.

Nancy was wandering aimlessly down an open hayfield, a mile from home, at two o'clock in the morning. She was walking parallel to Old Eagle Road, where we lived on. She was in her pajamas with her arm still extended in front of her.

A black Buick sedan slowed to a stop. Its driver watched in disbelief at a girl in her pajamas and her arm sticking out, walking through a field at two in the morning. *I remember her. She's that little bitch with the smart mouth. What in fuck is she doing? Could this be a trap? I should ignore her and just keep driving, but she looks so delicious! It looks too easy. There is an opening ahead. Where I can pass through and hide the car. I'll get out and see what's going on with her. I must be careful. She knows who I am. Where is that silly-looking mask?* He reached under the car seat and fished out the mask with the Mohawk Indian image.

He parked his car in the opening and got out. He looked around, but there were no car lights nor the sounds of car engines. He approached Nancy, from her side, who seemed totally oblivious of his presence. Without warning, he knocked her down and before she could regain consciousness, he gagged her with his bandana. He then dragged her deeper into the field from view of the road.

Clyde was driving through another gravel road perpendicular from the road the Buick was hid. Clyde couldn't wait any longer to urinate. He stopped his truck and got out. About halfway through his business, in the moonlight, he eyed some movement in the field about two hundred yards away. At first, he thought it was cattle, but there was no fence to keep them in. He heard a moan and he adjusted his eyes to clearly see someone dragging something. He stealthy walked closer, but still couldn't see clearly. So he stooped down and sneaked a little closer. Now, he was only about seventy-five yards away. He finally was able to clearly see a large man drag a body. Clyde froze in terror when the large man, wearing a Mohawk Indian mask, ran toward him. Clyde tripped and fell backward. The Mohawk man stood over Clyde as he lay on his back, defecating himself, and begging for his life.

"If it's not Mr. Bigshot from that shitty little dump of a bar who was showing off his money and letting everybody know what a big roller he is. You don't feel like such a big shot now, do you?" taunted the Mohawk man.

"Please," Clyde pleaded. "I won't tell anyone. I didn't see anything. I'll give you the money. Please, please. Let me go!"

Mohawk man loved the power he had over Clyde. He loved the begging. Adrenaline spun through him. He went berserk and beat Clyde to death despite his pleading. He was undecided what to do next. *He would have been a problem. He may have seen my car and identified it. He would have gone straight to the cops. I had no choice but to kill the old bastard.* He turned around and saw that the girl was still unconscious. Clyde's truck was parked in the road. Uncertain of the time, he worried about early-morning farmers with their tractors who will be passing through soon. No time to do the girl here. *Should I take her with me or leave her?* He looked around and noticed a faint headlight of a car in the distance. He was uncertain whether the car was coming in his direction, but it was enough to cause panic. Mohawk man ran back to his Buick and left Nancy and Clyde where they lay.

Nancy gained consciousness at the peak of dawn. Her head was throbbing where the Mohawk man punched her. She struggled but was unable to untie the bandana that was tight around her head and placed between her upper and lower jaw. She tried to get up but lost her balance and fell. *How did I get here?* The last thing she remembered was when she was in her bedroom. She looked around and saw something or someone lying on the ground just a few yards away. Her confusion turned to terror when she realized what lay motionless on the ground was a man with his head bashed in. All she could think of was to get away.

* * * * *

Randy Rose loved being the evening security guard at Robin's Tool & Dye plant. He took great pride in wearing his security uniform. He wore a gold-colored badge above his left chest pocket. He would strut through the shop floor, eyeing the evening labor force as they toiled.

He would stand guard at the door entrance and randomly check employees' lunchboxes, purses, and bags for stolen items or alcohol. Whenever an employee resisted search, Randy would point at his badge and give a lecture on his authority. Randy had found his niche.

When his shift was over at midnight, Randy would patrol the countryside searching for criminal acts of any kind. It wasn't an official job through the county, city, or even neighborhood watch. He just liked to do it. The folks around knew about Randy and his patrol, but they just joked about it. Authentic lawmen thought he was an oddball, but willingly tolerated him as long as he didn't try to make contact or harm anyone.

At two in the morning, Randy was doing a patrol and was about to call it quits for the night. He saw headlights in the distance coming toward him on Old Eagle Road. Then he saw the headlights off. That's not unusual if the vehicle was in a driveway, but it was clear that it was in the road or on the side of it. Randy turned off his own headlights and stealthily drove slowly toward that area. Suddenly, a different set of lights came on and a car pulled out of what seemed to be an open field. The car was coming directly in his direction. Randy turned his headlights on so the driver could see his car well in advance. As the car sped by, he recognized its make. It was a black Buick, but he was uncertain of its year. He turned around at the nearest crossroad to follow the car and get the numbers of the license plate, but its driver was going too fast to follow. *Probably someone stopped to take a leak, but why was he driving so fast? Why is he out here at two in the morning?*

*   *   *   *   *

No less than two dozen neighbors had congregated in our front yard to begin a search for Nancy, and more were coming in by the minute. Within thirty minutes, the crowd had swelled up to over fifty neighbors. Many had forgotten why they were here once they met other neighbors they haven't talked to in months.

Henrietta Cotton or "Mother Cotton" (everybody called her Mother Cotton) heard about the "missing person" alert on her citizen's band radio. It was stated that a search party was gathering at the Johnsons' place, and Mother Cotton didn't want to miss out. She hurriedly whipped up a large batch of sausage and biscuits to feed the volunteers. She would have drove her Studebaker up Old Eagle Road to our house, but there were scores of cars and pickup trucks that lined the road. She then decided to walk the one-quarter-mile distance. She underestimated how many would be volunteering. Her sausage and biscuits only fed a fraction of the crowd.

Gossip was thick concerning Nancy's issues, which had been spreading through the farming community all winter.

"I heard the girl was practicing witchcraft," claimed Clarence Jones, a lifelong resident.

"Well, I know for a fact that the whole dadgum family does it!" said Luke Cantrell, a known moonshiner.

Harold Hall, a widower, had no intention of joining in on the search. He was just here for the entertainment of others and to spread more malicious gossip. "We don't know a thing about these people. No telling what they're into."

While the crowd was forming in front of our house, to eventually be organized and broken up into crack search teams, there was another rumor that Ethel Judd also called the sheriff's department about Clyde, who didn't come home the night before. However, many in the crowd laughed at the notion. They assumed that Clyde probably got so drunk at the Blue Mule again and probably got lost driving home and was sleeping it off in his truck, no doubt.

*   *   *   *   *

Deputy Duke was exhausted from another graveyard shift. Usually, he'd hide his patrol car and take a nap for thirty minutes or so, to take the edge off. One of his favorite hiding places for a good snooze was under a billboard, advertising "Pete's Radiator Repair Service. A good place to take a leak!" However, there was no catching a few winks this time, for his patrol tonight was exceptionally busy. He had to break up a fight between Ralph Burns and Willie Brewer outside the Salty Dog Saloon. According to Willie, he caught his wife with Ralph in the backseat of his car. Deputy Duke arrested Sally Crawford, aka Southfield Sally, who typically solicited drivers on Southfield Street in Morris. So Duke was looking forward to the end of his night shift, when he received a call from the dispatcher about two missing-person reports.

"The sheriff is asking, as a favor, if you would continue your patrol until noon. Two locals have been reported missing. Stop by the office to pick up the reports and do a follow-up," requested Dispatcher Helen. "Over."

"I'm on my way. Over and out."

"If I'm to work until noon after working all night, then I've got to eat," grumbling, Deputy Duke was talking to himself. "After I pick up the missing-persons reports, then I'm taking a break and heading to Imogene's Corner Diner for some waffles first."

Duke knew that if one or both of the missing are not found within twenty-four hours, then an official report must be filed by the department. That would mean double shifts for all deputies, including him. He turned the corner and got on Old Eagle Road when he saw a pickup truck that didn't fit. He knew most, if not all the farmer's trucks in this area, and this one didn't look familiar. He did a check on the license plate, and it was registered to Clyde.

Duke stepped out of the patrol car. He suspected that Clyde could be sleeping in the cab, so he walked up to truck and looked through the side window and saw that it was empty. He turned slowly in a circle, looking into the horizon in an effort to see any sign of Clyde. Through the grass hay that stood over a foot appeared to be part of clothing peeking out, about two hundred yards away. *The remains of a scarecrow that had fallen on the ground?* He walked toward it and stopped. He saw that it was obviously not a scarecrow but a man he suspected was trying to hide. He grabbed his revolver but didn't pull it out of the holster. He shouted, "You there, laying down. Stand up and show yourself!" No movement. "I'm going to tell you one more time to slowly stand up with your back facing me and your hands out where I can see them. Do it now!" Still no movement. Duke cautiously walked closer until he was near enough to see Clyde's face shockingly beaten and forehead caved in, surrounded by a ghastly pool of blood. Deputy Duke leaned over and puked.

Sheriff Diller and Deputy Wilson arrived within ten minutes of Deputy Duke's call. They set up a perimeter around the scene and called Detective Summers and Booker to collect forensic evidence, including outsole impressions. The lab results of Billy Allen's impressions, which were taken from his shoes, did not match the samples that were collected in the blood-splattered floor of the Jeb and Sally Howard double murder. Billy was cleared as a possible suspect. The law officials were interested in discovering if this murder was connected to the one of Jeb and Sally Howard. Clyde's body was taken to the medical examiner's lab, although it could not be officially identified until an examination and confirmation by the next of kin. Deputy Wilson drove to his home to break the news to Ethel, Clyde's wife, about the man found in the hayfield, who was suspected to be her husband. The Deputy drove Ethel, who was hysterical, to come the examiners lab to confirm his identity.

When Randy awakened at midmorning, he turned his General Electric AM transistor radio on to the WAKE Morris Radio station. On its news segment, he was stunned to hear the news about the murder of Clyde Judd. *The announcer said that Clyde was found in a field on Old Eagle Road. That's where I was last night.* He called the sheriff's department to report the black Buick he witnessed speeding by him. Helen, the dispatcher, took Randy's call.

Helen King had heard it all in her seven years of service as a dispatcher for the sheriff's department. Most residents call to report loud music, domestic disputes, or burglaries. One of her most hilarious calls was from Fred Tuddle, whose portly wife was stuck in the washtub. Randy was her most frequent caller. Every few weeks and even sooner, he was calling in to report strangers walking on the side of the road or partying teenagers congregating on backroads When she received a call from Randy about a car speeding on Old Eagle Road at two o'clock in the morning, on a normal night, she would have taken his call seriously, like several of his previous calls. This one was different because it was allegedly near the scene of Judd's homicide.

Sheriff Diller paid Randy a visit at his mother's home as a follow-up on his call to the station. After quizzing Randy on what he saw in the early-morning hours, he seemed confused as to what kind of car he'd seen and its actual location. Randy claimed the headlight on the passenger side was dimmed and was likely going bad. Nonetheless, Diller instructed his deputies to keep a search of suspicious drivers of black Buicks. They were common make of cars on the roads of that day. He also gathered the names of owners of Buicks at the vehicle licensing office for the county.

CHAPTER ELEVEN

"**I** DON'T CARE if the cows need tending to. It can wait another day," grumbled Freddy.

"Well, when I was in the back hanging laundry, I saw one cow that looked sick. One of its eyes looked terrible. That poor thang looked like it was suffering. Your dad expects you take care of it today. He told you last night, when he was here, about the work he needed done," complained Ellen, Freddy's wife.

"It's pink eye. I'll spray her eye and give her a shot tomorrow. I bought a new Winchester yesterday and I wanna go shoot it."

"We can't afford you buying another gun! You got too many guns. We don't have the money for you to buy more of those guns. Take it back!"

"Dammit, Ellen! We talked about his. I gotta buy all the guns I can before the damn liberals put a stop to it!"

"You're out of your mind, Freddy. That ain't gonna happen. You been talking to your crazy cousin too much. He never was right. Now, stop playing around with those guns before you shoot yourself. Stop acting like a child and grow up!"

"We need to protect ourselves. Whoever killed Jeb and Sally might come after us next. We gotta be ready!" Freddy walked out the back door and closed it before Ellen had a chance to reply.

Ellen was enraged that Freddy would have the audacity to walk out the door and close it while she was reprimanding him. *What's gotten into him?* She reopened the back door and started shouting at Freddy. "We gonna live in this shitty little trailer for the rest of our lives? Why don't you do something with your life? If you would take more of an interest in your dad's farm, then maybe, just maybe, he'll give you a raise or even make you a partner. But hell no, not you. You're just gallivanting off with your damn gun when you have responsibilities. Freddy, are you listening to me? Freddy? Freddy, turn around when I'm talking to you! Freddy? Stop walking away from me!" Freddy knew he would have to face Ellen's wrath when he returned home, but for now, all he could think about was being alone. Away from his nag for a wife. Away from his monster of a father.

Whenever Freddy had a gun in his hand, his alternate self took over. He was no longer "Freddy the Freeloader," the nickname his drinking buddies gave him, after the character in the "Red Skelton Show." He was no longer Freddie, the henpecked husband. He is no longer Freddy, who had never lived more than a quarter of a mile from his parents' house. He could forget that he lived in a trailer on his overbearing dad's farm, and that he was actually only one of his dad's farmhands. When Freddy was alone and carrying a gun in the great outdoors, he was sometimes transformed into Marshall Dillon, confronting a desperate gunslinger to save Dodge City. At least in his own mind. Other times he would have the grand illusion that he was Wyatt Earp, taming the West. Being outside, far enough away from Ethel, his father, or reality, this was his only escape from the real world.

The farther away that Freddy walked, the more at peace that he felt. Freddy didn't hunt game. He didn't shoot living creatures at all, unless it was a poisonous snake, which was rare. He only liked to target practice. He would set up cans and bottles to shoot. He would sit for hours and daydream as the world passed him by. *I'm a total failure. I live a meager existence. I hate my life.* That was all about to change for Freddy Ellis.

Freddy pondered his future and saw no hope. He positioned the tip of the barrel in his mouth. He struggled to reach the trigger with a finger or thumb but could barely touch it. So he pulled his sock and shoe off and placed his big toe against the trigger. *At least I'll die by a Winchester 94 30-30. I'll go out in style.* Then he heard the sound of something moving through leaves at the edge of the woods. *Probably a squirrel or rabbit,* he thought. Then he saw what appeared to be a girl's face peeking at him from behind a tree. He pulled the rifle out of his mouth and stood up. The girl began backing away. "What are you doing over there? Do you work for my dad?" She just stood there staring back at him. She was too far away for Freddy to see well. *What's that covering her mouth?* Nancy was still gagged by the bandana between her upper and lower jaw, which she had been unable to loosen. "Who are you?" Nancy looked at Freddy's gun with suspicion, so he put it on the ground to ease her fear. "I need to get that off your mouth. I won't hurt you." Nancy was reluctant to allow him to come closer but finally cooperated as he cut the bandana off with his pocket knife. "What happened to you? Who did this to you? Where do you live? I'll take you back to my place and I'll call the sheriff. Come on with me." He took her by the arm. She winced when Freddy picked up the rifle, so he put in back on the ground and left it behind as he continued helping her along.

Ellen was standing at the back door as Freddy and Nancy approached the house. "Who is that, Freddy?" Ellen asked.

"I don't know. Found her in the woods. Her mouth was tied up. She needs help. Call somebody. The sheriff . . .call the sheriff."

"Her mouth tied up? What are you talking about, Freddy? She's so dirty looking. She's wearing pajamas. Why would she be in the woods, wearing pajamas? Where did she come from?"

"She needs help! Get her some water, and I'll call Diller."

An ambulance arrived just as Sheriff Diller was exiting his squad car outside Freddy and Ellen Ellis's home. Then two more deputy sheriff patrol cars were there. A fire truck from the Morris Volunteer Fire Department rolled in for good measure too. As Nancy was treated at the scene, Diller was taking Freddy's statement. Cub reporter Max Miller of the *Morris Gazette* arrived to interview Freddy, and he was desperate for a hot scoop.

Deputy Duke was sent to our home to disperse the crowd of volunteers and gawkers. Their cars and trucks lined both sides of the narrow gravel road. Duke used the loudspeaker in his patrol car to ask everybody to return to their vehicles and to exit the area in an orderly fashion.

My parents had been going out of their minds over Nancy's disappearance, and to express that they were overjoyed at the news is a huge understatement. We were at the emergency room when the ambulance arrived at the Morris Memorial Hospital. We were told that my sister was in a state of shock but seemed physically okay. After she was physical examined, Nancy was admitted overnight for observation. Sheriff Diller and the state detectives were unable to gather any facts from Nancy. The trauma she had endured caused her speech to be incoherent. We were finally permitted to visit her, but she continued to talk gibberish.

"I have to know, Doctor. Was my daughter raped?" Mom asked nervously.

"There is no evidence of sexual violation. She's been through a very traumatic ordeal that no child should have to go through. We will watch her closely tonight. If all is well, then let's get her admitted to our mental facility, and we'll go from there. We have an excellent staff there that will give her the best care. It's exactly where she should be."

"How long will they keep her at the facility?" my dad asked.

"It's difficult to say," answered the physician. "Whenever a child has been assaulted, a mental evaluation is procedural. Your daughter seems to have no memory of what happened, and she's extremely incoherent in her speech. This is likely temporary. Our staff should be able to help her recover more rapidly. Try not to worry."

Throughout the evening, Nancy continued to talk to herself incoherently and was nervously shaking. A nurse gave Nancy a mild sedative, but it did little to calm her. Finally, a heavier dose put Nancy into a deep sleep. She was slowly spiraling downward. Below her, she could see a hayfield. As she continued to float downward, should could see a human figure looking upward, as if waiting for her. Getting closer and closer, she could make out clearer details. It was a large man, but there was something about his face. A demented-looking face or a mask . . . it's the scary man in the scary mask! Nancy awakened in a screeching and piercing cry.

* * * * *

The next day, the front-page headlines in the *Morris Gazette* read: Freddy Ellis Rescues Young Teen from Assault. The entire first page of the *Gazette* detailed Freddy's heroism in leading Nancy away from an unknown assailant, who was still at large. Afterward, it seemed that reporters from all the major newspapers and television news networks statewide were interested in Freddy's story. He spent the next three days doing interviews. The story caught the attention of the *New York Times, Los Angeles Times,* and other big-name newspapers. All three television stations–ABC, CBS, and NBC–reported the story on their nightly news. Walter Cronkite did a news special. A representative for the *Tonight Show* called Freddy to appear as a guest with Johnny Carson. Other talk shows followed. By the end of the week, Freddy Ellis was a national sensation.

* * * * *

Mohawk man was pacing. *I fucked up. Why couldn't I just keep driving? That smart-mouthed girl wasn't worth it. What was that farmer doing there? I got his money, but it's not worth it. Nobody ever drives through there that early. I had to kill him. What choice did I have? He may have had a gun. I can't worry about that now. What's done is done. The cops have nothing.*

CHAPTER TWELVE

T HE BODY FOUND in the hayfield on Old Eagle Road was indeed confirmed to be Clyde Judd and later identified by his wife, Ethel. Outsole impressions of shoe prints on the blood-soaked ground were collected. The analysis identified the impressions to be a match of the ones found on Jeb and Sally Howard's floor as suspected. The lawmen coordinated a statewide manhunt. A swarm of all available units saturated the immediate area. All were working twelve- and even sixteen-hour shifts. The sheriff's department solicited help from the public in locating the murderer. They broadcasted, on television and radio, a description based on the information gathered, which mostly included the height and weight of the assailant. Lawmen also went door-to-door to residents, asking for help.

Sheriff Diller stopped by Ethel's home for an interview. He intended to gather facts that would help retrace Clyde's steps during the hours prior to his death. Ethel had always put on airs about Clyde and his bad habits. She would drag Clyde to church every Sunday morning, regardless of his brutal hangovers. Whenever the other dedicated and judgmental church ladies would comment about Clyde's nodding off during services, Ethel would always give the same excuse. "Clyde works so hard all week and Saturdays. He's so tired Sunday morning," she would say. When quizzed by the sheriff, she was reluctant to admit to Clyde's drinking habits and his visits to honky-tonks. She knew Clyde would frequent the Blue Mule on weekends, but it was rarely on weekdays, when Clyde was murdered. After Ethel's admission about her suspicions of Clyde's whereabouts, the sheriff's next stop was the Blue Mule.

As Sheriff Diller stood inside the front door, he looked around at the small gathering, including familiar troublemakers who keep the night patrol busy. The sheriff was amused how there was always one or two patrons who would attempt to hide their drinks whenever he entered a bar. He walked over to where a bartender stood polishing glasses. This was a habit that barkeeps do to look busy.

"Is your name Alvin?" the sheriff asked. That was a name that Ethel gave him. She remembered Clyde mentioning Alvin while in one of his alcohol-induced stupors.

"That's me," Alvin responded in a meek voice as he felt as if his bowels would to water. His brother convinced him to hide a truck load of stolen batteries in his barn and Alvin has been a bundle of nerves ever since.

The sheriff showed Alvin a picture of Clyde and asked if he was at the Blue Mule on the morning of his death. Alvin was relieved that Diller wasn't there about stolen batteries. However, he didn't want the hassle of being a witness in a murder case, but he thought it was better than to lie to a law officer and get caught. "Yes, he was here." He acknowledged that Clyde Judd was at the establishment that night and had lots of money that he was flashing. "When I heard about Clyde being murdered, I assumed that robbery may have been a motive."

"Did anyone else notice that Mr. Judd had money?"

Alvin gathered his thoughts. "There was one feller. I've never saw him before that night. He was tall. He was big and stout. He noticed that Clyde had wad of dough. The reason he stuck in my mind is that I keep my eye on strangers that come in here. Especially the big 'uns. If they cause trouble, then it could be a problem for me controlling the situation."

When Diller returned to his office and began to connect what he knew, he reflected on Mary Weaver's description of the man she saw crossing in the cornfield. *The man was as big as one of those wrestlers I see on TV, and he was tall!* This is the same cornfield that was adjacent to Jeb and Sally's land. Diller thought it intriguing that Alvin, the bartender, gave a similar description of a patron in his bar that stood out. *He was tall. He was big and stout. He was eyeing Clyde Judd and his money pouch on the same night that he was murdered.* What made the puzzle even more interesting was that Nancy Johnson was apparently found only about a mile from Clyde's body. It was estimated that her abduction attempt occurred approximately at the same time Clyde was murdered.

Lawmen investigated Nancy's alleged abduction where Freddy found her, a mile from the murder scene of Clyde. There were no suspects in her ordeal yet, but it was thought to be committed by the same perpetrator.

Detectives' reenactment revealed that Nancy may have been sleepwalking. She encountered an assailant who gagged her with the intention of rape. The assailant was surprised by Clyde Judd, who stopped his truck to urinate. A puddle of it was found by the truck. The detectives speculated that the perpetrator attacked Judd to rob him or kill him because he witnessed an abduction in process.

Early the next week, Nancy was showing some signs of improvement in her mental state. The sheriff and other lawmen were keeping close contact with Dr. Rice, the psychiatrist assigned to treat Nancy. He was to report to the sheriff when Nancy was recovered enough to communicate rationally.

"Miss Johnson still has a lengthy recovery time," Dr. Rice informed the sheriff, "but she is talking. She knows who I am, and she can answer simple question. That's an improvement, but she is suffering from severe amnesia."

"I would like to try and talk to her," Sheriff Diller requested.

"Please, only for a few moments. Trying to relay the traumatic ordeal could result in a relapse."

"She can possibly give a description of the scumbag who did this to her. He's the same perpetrator who killed an elderly couple. I'll be gentle. Relax, Doc."

Nancy's wrists were no longer restrained to her bed railing to prevent her from injuring herself at night as she slept. Her nightmares had subsided with properly administered drugs. The restraints remained off, unless she started fighting the orderlies again during her late-night screaming spells.

The sheriff entered Nancy's room. He was a seasoned lawman, but even he was stunned at her demented expression. "Hello, Nancy." His greeting was as nonconfrontational as he could muster. Nancy looked at him with a fixed, vacant expression. "Can you describe the person who restrained you?" She just stared at the sheriff and said nothing. "Do you know the name of the person? Just nod your head if you know who gagged you, Nancy?"

Nancy's thoughts began racing wildly. She could no longer differentiate among reality, dreams, and delusions. As if an out-of-body experience, a woman was dragging her away. She was overcome with dread and unspeakable terror. She was being pulled farther and farther away from the security of her bedroom and safety of home. Her mind flashed. She was staring upward at a man. His face was covered with a mask. He stood over her and groping her crotch. He began dragging her.

"Nancy? Can you hear me, Nancy?" the sheriff's voice jarred Nancy from a trancelike state. She began shouting incoherently as reality settled in. An orderly, who was at the nurse's station just outside her room, rushed in. Then a nurse entered and asked the sheriff to step outside as she and the orderly tended to Nancy.

Later that same day, a secretary at the hospital's administration office called our home. Mom picked up the telephone receiver and was asked to arrange an appointment with Dr. Rice to discuss Nancy's condition, preferably that same day. In the privacy of Dr. Rice's office, he informed my parents that Nancy's impatient stay at the psychiatric facility could be long term. The doctor said that Nancy had developed schizophrenia. He explained this psychotic disorder is characterized by her strange speech, her inability to understand reality, and hearing voices.

"It's unfortunate this condition has appeared during your daughter's most crucial years," explained Dr. Rice.

"Can it be controlled?" Dad asked.

"Yes, with continued psychological evaluation. There will be a combination of treatments depending on what works best for her. There will be a team approach, with various specialists, so we can be sure all her medical, psychological, and social needs are inevitably filled. We will do everything possible to make sure she can, one day, live a normal life."

"She's alive, at least," Dad said.

"Considering all, she's extremely lucky to be alive," added Dr. Rice.

*   *   *   *   *

"What you plan to do with your life, boy?" Everett asked Larry directly as he sat on the couch, smoking a cigarette. Violet was outside, in the garden. Everett was finally alone with Larry and seized the chance to confront him.

"What do ya' mean?" Larry replied. He turned his head toward the kitchen, hoping Violet would rush in to rescue him from Everett's scorn.

"She's not in there, son. Your momma is outside. It's just me and you. We are going to have a talk," Everett said with a smirk. "What are you, nineteen? Just sittin' around, doing nothing all day. What do ya' plan to do with yourself?"

"I've got plans. I don't have to tell you nothing." Larry started to get up as if to exit the front door, but Everett pushed him back onto the couch.

"Answer me, boy," Everett demanded.

"I plan to get a job," Larry lied.

"Oh yeah, doing what? Where do you plan to get a job at?"

"Around."

"Tell me the truth about this Jerry guy. What's going on between you two?"

"You know he adopted me!"

"If he adopted you, then why ain't you living with him?"

"His place ain't big enough. His landlord won't allow more than one living there. He's saving for a bigger place."

"You little sissy boy. He didn't adopt you. I had it checked out at the agency. Those papers are fake. I ain't told your mom yet. Jerry, or whatever he calls himself, just wants to keep you as his punk, whenever he wants you."

"It ain't like that!" Larry ran out of the house to the safety of his mother.

"I better not ever see you two sleeping together under my roof, ever again!" Everett shouted as Larry exited.

CHAPTER THIRTEEN

SHERIFF DILLER WAS under mounting pressure. There were three murders and no suspects. During Diller's election campaign, he promised the citizens of Morris that if they elected him, he would deliver a secure and safe community. He promised an elite and professional team of law enforcement officers and staff. He was amused at the fact that Morris was already safe and secure. Violent crimes were extremely rare, and folks were comfortable leaving their doors unlocked, day or night, at home or away. So, for Diller, running for a first term in office, his promises to the voters were a given. To his advantage, Diller looked like a sheriff. His supporters were so taken by his charm and charisma. Donations to his campaign outflanked the incumbent of twenty years, three to one. After an anticipated victorious sweep in the election, Diller's opponents accused his campaign of buying the sheriff's seat. They had given him the nickname "Stealer Diller," because they said he stole the election.

Another election year loomed, and the residents were afraid to go outside their own homes at night. The sale of guns was on the rise for self-protection. Residents were calling the sheriff's office, requesting and even demanding heavier patrols of their streets. Usually, the locals of Morris would blame outsiders or out-of-towners when a crime of almost any caliber occurred. However, these murders were thought to be committed by one of our own. This fear was causing a distrust of each other in area. The three homicides, under Diller's watch, had followed years of peace and tranquility prior to his election. His opponents began to label him with the name "Killer Diller."

Phone tips were coming in, from all over, from witnesses who claim they had information that may help nab the killer. Some were legitimately trying to report what they knew and others were prank callers. Most were investigated. Mrs. Hornbuckle was outside of her home getting clothes off the line. She called the sheriff to report that she saw a man walk around on the other side of her house. She said that she hid behind the bedsheets that were hanging on the clothesline until she felt it was safe to hurry back into her house. She feared the man that walked by could have been the killer, looking for another victim. She gave a full description, but it was discovered that the man was actually a meter reader for the water department. The night dispatcher at the sheriff's office received an anonymous call from someone who claimed to be driving slowly, with the windows down, and heard screaming. The caller said it was coming from inside a home, while driving by. When it was checked out, it was discovered to be a domestic dispute. Herman and Doris Hamer were bickering again. The dispatcher knew the anonymous caller was Melvin Long, who was thought to be a bit of a kook by everyone down at the precinct. She didn't want to let on for fear Melvin would hang up the phone. The way the homicide cases were dragging, every lead was needed. All the calls received turned up dry. Most of the evidence the officials had was already gathered at the crime scenes, and there was little progress since.

*   *   *   *   *

Nancy was standing in an open farm field. The sun had an indescribable glow. It wasn't terribly bright in a way that would make you squint. It was more of a radiance that made the countryside stunningly beautiful. She was in awe of the grass, trees, and even the mountains in the horizon. She could hear nature as if for the first time. *Why have I not noticed the beauty of nature before?* It was if she could hear each individual bird in its own distinct sound, but all of them seemed to sing in perfect harmony. She listened with fascination at the sounds of insects. Then Nancy became confused. *Why am I here? How did I get here? Shouldn't I be somewhere else? I should be in school. I don't belong here.* The surroundings were swiftly becoming dark. *God help me. I don't want to be here.* She was overcome with an unimaginable feeling of dread. *God, please help me. Help me . . . help me . . . help me.* She saw movement in a wooded area several hundred feet away. Then she saw the hair. The floating hair. *It's her. Please, no. She's here for me. Please God. Make her go away.* Her blood red, contemptuous eyes were locked on Nancy's. As she moved closer, she began to grin, to show dozens of ghastly looking pointed teeth. She extended her hand. "Take my hand, Nancy." Nancy resisted with what little control the bell witch had not taken from her. "Take my hand and come with me, Nancy. Take my hand. Take my hand."

An orderly was on each side of the hospital bed strapping Nancy's arms. A third orderly was turning Nancy on her side, while a nurse flipped up her gown to administer a shot in her butt cheek. Nancy was screaming in horror but had not yet awakened.

The bell witch had a death grip on Nancy's wrist. They were floating through the air. She had her eyes locked on Nancy. It was as if Nancy could feel the bell witches' eyes speak, and it was like they were saying, "Wait until you see this, Nancy, and you are going to hate it." They were spiraling downward until they were on the ground. The first thing that Nancy saw was Zoomer. *You're alive! My Zoomer is alive!* Zoomer looked back at Nancy and his tail began to wag. She heard his same familiar bark. Zoomer was overjoyed to see her. She called for him, but he remained standing in the same spot in the middle of a gravel road. *Road . . . Zoomer's in the road! Zoomer . . . Zoomer!* Nancy could hear the sound of Zoomer's bones crushing under the impact of a car as it passed over. The bell witch with a monstrous laugh kept her grip. Zoomer reared up his mangled head. With a fixed look upon Nancy, he made a sound that can only be described as the voice of Satan.

Nancy's arms jerked against the restraints. She looked up at the nurse. She was confusing her dreams with reality and vice-versa. She didn't know difference anymore. *Did I just have a dream about Zoomer or did I really just see him?* She looked at her straps. She began to panic. *They tied me up again. Am I dreaming now?*

"It's okay, honey," said Nurse Dexter. "Just relax. Relax, honey! It was just a dream. We'll take off the straps later. Just relax, please." The nurse was sitting with Nancy until the sedative calmed her and induced a more relaxed sleep.

CHAPTER FOURTEEN

SUMMER BREAK FROM school had finally arrived. At last, I had total freedom to care for and ride Sam. There was, at least, one downside to having a horse. Dad assigned me the duty of shoveling manure out of the stall. I dumped it in burlap sacks to be used to fertilize the garden. This was my least favorite task, but I took more pride in his feeding and grooming. I was also anxious to spend more time fishing in our pond. My parents bought me a brand-new Zebco rod and reel. It was a gift for getting good grades in the new school, and for just being such a swell kid, no doubt.

Dad bought a used tractor, equipped with a plow and a disk. He promised to teach me how to drive the tractor so I could eventually help with tilling the ground that I soon regretted. I found that plowing was actually hard work. Disking the soil until it became soft was easier, but it was also monotonous. Circling the field on a tractor all day long turned out not to be my idea of summer fun.

Dad's new job was working out very well. He enjoyed a promotion in the past year, home every evening, and he had better health insurance. This was a tremendous help in getting treatment and therapy for Nancy.

My parents had another meeting with Dr. Rice, who informed them of her progress and setbacks. The doctor urged them to consent to a longer-than-expected in-patient stay. He said Nancy continued to suffer from paranoia, hallucinations, and the inability to recognize the difference between her dreams and reality. During our counseling sessions, other personalities emerge.

Sometimes she becomes a young child. Other times she becomes sinister and threatening. He also feared that Nancy is suicidal and should be guarded. With a little urging, they consented.

Their next stop was with Mr. Henson, the school counselor. He said that Nancy academically failed the ninth grade due to poor grades and excessive absence. However, considering her hospitalization, her grades could be reevaluated and rescinded through summer tutoring. My parents doubted that Nancy could endure the pressure of being tutored, under her circumstance, but were not giving up hope.

*　*　*　*　*

Jerry was ecstatic when he received a call from Jeremy Hill, the manager for Hillside Apartments. Jerry had been living in a small mother-in-law-apartment or, legally, an "accessory dwelling unit," for three years, but soon that will change. Hill informed Jerry that his leasing application was accepted. Jerry had been strapped for cash but finally raised enough that satisfied the required two months' down rent for lease. It's not what he really wanted for Larry and himself, but it's better than living under the watchful eye of Bertha Scott, his landlady. Her rules were ridiculously too picky. It was more like a jail sometimes. In fact, jail would certainly be a better alternative. She forbade him from having any guest after 10 pm, and women were off limits. "Absolutely no women allowed, Mr. Stanton," she had warned him before she gave him the keys for the apartment. "No drinking either!" What frustrated him the most is that no other tenants were allowed to live with him, and that included Larry, his son!

A jubilant Jerry called Larry with the news. "We'll finally be together."

"When can I move in?" Larry asked.

"I have the key now. We can move tomorrow. I'll stop by about eleven o'clock to get you and take you there. So pack your things tonight."

"Momma, help me pack. I gonna live with Dad. He'll be here in the morning."

"You'll do no such thing!" Violet protested. "I don't want you going with him!"

"You can't tell me what to do! I'm leaving tomorrow. I'm living with my dad!"

"I'm sorry I ever let you and him talk me into signing those darn adoption papers. Larry? I need to talk to ya, honey. Sit down a minute." Larry and Violet sat at the kitchen table. "Larry honey, are you doing dirty things with Jerry?" Larry looked down at the table's surface. "Larry, I'm your momma. You can tell me, sweetness."

Larry jumped up from the table. "He just loves me! He's like a real dad to me. I'll have more freedom with him than here living with Everett. It's just for a while anyway."

"Larry, I messed up. It was a mistake letting him adopt you. It don't matter now, no way. You're nineteen now, honey. It's weird you going to live with him. Everett said . . ."

"Everett's not my dad," Larry interrupted. "I can't live with him!"

Everett had walked in the front door and was listening. "Let him go on and shack up with Jerry, Violet!" Everett said as he entered the kitchen.

"Now, look what ya did, you old bitch. Look what ya did. You got Everett started now!" Larry yelled.

"Hey!" Everett shouted back as Violet began to cry. "You better watch your tongue! You're the only bitch around here. You're that damn Jerry's little bitch! I've been on to you two butt buddies all along. You wanna go have a disgusting life like that, then go ahead. It ain't nothing to me. I don't give a shit what ya'll do, but it's not gonna be here. I'll be glad to get rid of your lazy ass."

Larry was too mortified to reply. He just left the room without another word and avoided Everett for the rest of the day. Violet packed all of Larry's things and laid everything that he owned by the living room door. Jerry picked him up the next day.

CHAPTER FIFTEEN

NANCY REMAINED IN the mental ward for the entire summer. She had become well enough to stay focused during her tutoring sessions, and upon reevaluating her academic progress, the school administrator allowed her to pass to the next grade. In August, just before school began, Nancy was released in care of our parents.

Nancy sat quietly at the back seat as Dad drove her home. Mom, who was in the passenger side, turned slightly to her left to extend her left arm as she and Nancy held hands. I stayed home so that Nancy could feel free to talk to our parents if she felt the need.

Since Nancy was away, some remodeling was done to our house. It looked presentable enough that Nancy complimented the work. "We painted your room, Nancy," Mom said. She held her hand up to her mouth. "Oops! I let it slip. I wanted it to be a surprise. I'm sorry, Nancy." Mom never could keep things secret.

"What color is it?" Nancy asked meekly.

"It's pink."

"That's my favorite color."

"We hope you like it, Nancy," Dad said. "Welcome home, sweetheart."

"I'm so glad to be out of that place. I'm hungry. What's for dinner?"

They were standing on the front porch. "Well, why don't we go eat at your favorite restaurant, just as soon as you get settled? How would you like that?"

"Bernie's? There's no Bernie's around here."

"There is now," Dad said. "There is a new Bernie's restaurant franchise in Morris. It just opened."

They went inside and Nancy noticed it looked just as nice as the outside. The living room was painted a soft cream. Nancy walked into her room and loved the new color. She was pleasingly surprised to see that a new bedroom suit was added too–that surprise, my mom was able to keep quiet about. They even installed new doors on all the bedrooms since the old one looked as if they were added when the house was built. Nancy closed her bedroom door and noticed there was no lock on it. It only took a minute before she realized there was no mirror on her bedroom dresser. She tried to apply the methods that she learned to help overcome her feelings of persecution. She shook it off and returned to the living room. I shared my summer activities with her until our parents finished getting refreshed for the restaurant. They gave me strict orders not to bring up the subject of her stay at the hospital. However, Nancy did talk about it some, but I only listened.

Just before we left for the restaurant, Nancy went to use the bathroom and looked at herself in the mirror. She felt a twinge of nervousness as she reflected on her delusions and nightmares. She remembered what Dr. Rice taught her about maintaining positive thoughts and reminded herself that witches don't exist. What she had experienced was in her imagination. Her dreams are not real but just in her subconscious.

Our family sat in the restaurant, and we had just ordered our food when Nancy noticed Brad sitting at another table. He turned to glance at her, but then he looked away. Nancy was relieved that Brad would not be attending school this year since he had already graduated. She also hoped that he would be attending college far enough away that he would not be coming home. If he came home to his parents on weekends, then he would be attending church. The one we attended as well as his family. Nancy hoped she would never see Brad ever again.

Nancy excused herself to visit the restroom and just as she started to enter, she heard Brad's voice. "Nancy?"

She turned around. "Hi, Brad."

"It's good to see you, Nancy. I just want to tell you that I'm sorry."

"You don't have to, Brad. You don't have to say nothing else to me. You're just a boy. Boys will be boys. I thought you were more mature. You will eventually grow up or, at least, I hope you do. We have nothing more to say to each other. I forgive you, Brad. I really do. I want you to know that. Goodbye, Brad." She turned and walked into the restroom. When she came out, Brad had left the restaurant.

Sunday morning as we attended church services, several of the parishioners greeted Nancy with a hug and welcomed her return. The Pastor Elmer Ross spoke of God's love and how we are not alone. Nancy listened as the pastor expressed the need to place all our burdens in God's hands and accepting his son, Jesus Christ, as our savior.

At the end of service, the pastor asked the congregation to stand. As the organ music played softly, he asked if anyone who has not made that decision to do so could come forward. Nancy stepped out from the pew and walked to the altar where the pastor waited. They prayed silently and talked for several moments while the organ continued. Nancy experienced a feeling of joy that she had not had before as the burden of her problems were lifted.

*   *   *   *   *

School would be starting in less than a week, and Nancy was determined to make a fresh start. She was reading again. She was planning her course of study. She intended to be at the top of her class. Her positive self-esteem was returning. She was aware of the challenge of her mental disease and was ready to meet it.

The first day of school had arrived. Nancy sat nervously in the bus, unsure how the other students will react to her. Nancy put on her game face and smiled at Angie when she got on the bus and was walking down the aisle toward us. They each greeted as if nothing had happened. One by one, the rest of the students got on as Mr. Jones made his rounds.

Nancy absorbed the lessons taught in all her classes that first morning of school. At lunch break, she was sitting in the cafeteria with Angie and other students. They were all talking about their summer festivities. She feared someone would ask her about her summer or her problem, but no one did. Nonetheless, she was prepared for any comment. She was not going to let anyone or anything get her down.

"I met this great guy over the summer. His name is Charlies Drucker, and he kept looking at me at Louie's Diner. He had the waitress bring me over a malt. Then he just came right over and started talking to me. We been seeing each other almost every day. He's a senior this year!" chirped Lisa.

"He had the waitress bring you a malt and he paid for it? That's so romantic!" said Lucy. "I broke up with Johnny. Remember him, Angie, the guy I met at your sleepover last year?" Lucy put her hand over her mouth and looked at Nancy. "I'm sorry, Nancy. I shouldn't have mentioned the . . ."

Nancy spoke up before Lucy finished the sentence. "Why be sorry? I'm just sorry things didn't work out for you and Johnny. There's more than one fish in the sea, Lucy. I saw some new guys in my classes this morning. Imagine the possibilities." Nancy laughed at her own comment and all the other girls laughed with her. Nancy not only survived her first real social hurdle upon her return, she aced it with style and class.

During the first week of school, Nancy keep hearing talk about the teacher who had fallen in the hall last year. She began having unexplained flashbacks that she couldn't connect to anything.

"Poor Miss Pruitt. I still can't believe she's gone," commented Annie in the cafeteria.

"I miss talking to her at the library during study hall," added Teresa. "She was so sweet."

"I sure like her better than the new librarian, old Mrs. Brian. She's so crabby," said Annie.

Nancy couldn't erase it from her thoughts. She finally felt she had to find out more of what happened to Miss Pruitt. She asked her homeroom teacher about the details, including where Pruitt had her accident.

"Oh, the poor thing was lying in hallway during class time," said Mrs. Tucker. "Nobody saw her fall. They say she just tripped and banged her head. She was lying on the floor of a doorway. She never recovered. She died after a few months in the nursing home. She was going to retire soon too. It was such a tragic end to one of the most wonderful teachers that I've ever had the pleasure to work with. She is really missed around here."

"She was lying at a doorway?" Nancy asked.

"Her head was in the hallway and her lower portion was in the room. It was if she was walking out of the room and fell."

"Do you remember the room number, Mrs. Tucker?"

"It was one of our math rooms, dear. Room 203. Why are you asking, honey?"

"No special reason. Just curious. I remember her from the library."

Nancy decided to go to the section where Miss Pruitt fell. Sporadic flashbacks of events from last year was going through her mind. Dr. Rice said that she may begin to remember unpleasant thoughts that are mentally repressed. He explained that her emotions of dealing with traumatic events can become too much for her memory processing. This will lead to repression of the memory.

Nancy stared at the classroom door. She slowly opened it and looked in. Like a jolt, the memories of painful events flooded her mind. She remembered her feelings of paranoia. *Have I been in here before or was it a dream?* She stepped in and inquisitively walked through. As if she was floating, just below the ceiling, in an out-of-body way, she looked down at herself. The room was dark. Someone walked in and Nancy saw herself, below, become startled and in a panic, bolting out. She saw herself collide with a woman, who fell. The memory was very vivid now. It wasn't a dream conjured by her imagination. It was real, and she knew she was responsible for Miss Pruitt's injury and death.

Nancy finished the school day, preoccupied with the memory that she had blocked. She was contemplating whether to come forward and confess her deed or to keep it a secret. By the end of the school day, she knew that she could never overcome the guilt of this by keeping quiet. She had an appointment with Dr. Rice for a therapy session on the next day and decided to tell him everything.

Dr. Rice has had two previous clients to confess serious crimes involving homicide. In both incidents, the clients were reluctant to turn themselves in or contact their attorney. By law, Dr. Rice was required to report such confessions that involved alleged murder. Client confidentiality did not apply in murder cases. He was unsure about Nancy's incident with Miss Pruitt, since it could be determined to be an accident. Nancy wanted to come clean, so she agreed to have my parents come to his office to inform them of her predicament.

Dr. Rice met with my parents and Nancy on that very same day. They all decided the best plan was to speak to Sheriff Diller. Within a week, the district attorney and Nancy, with her attorney, met in the county's criminal court judge to settle the matter. In an official court hearing the following Monday, the judge decided that no charges would be filed and the case was dismissed.

CHAPTER SIXTEEN

"**I** WANT YOU to come home this weekend, Larry. Your grandpa will be visiting from Hixson and he'll want the whole family here," Violet pleaded. "You know it don't make a hill of beans what Everett thinks. He's ain't gonna bother you. Pay him no mind. You just come on over."

"I'm not comin' unless my dad can come too. Besides, he'll have to drive me," Larry replied.

"Can't Jerry just bring you here and come and git you later?"

"If he ain't comin', I ain't comin'!"

Violet was worried that her father, Donnie Jackson, a stern and judgmental disciplinarian, would scorn Larry and Jerry. Violet had not informed him of the adoption, and she feared that he wouldn't approve. Violet thought it would be impossible to keep it a secret during his weeklong visit. Larry, Everett, Tommy, or her sister, June, would surely spill the beans. Her father would question Jerry's presence if he was sitting at the table at their Sunday dinner or any time during his visit. Her father may even be suspicious of Larry and Jerry for other reasons aside from a thirty-something-year-old man adopting a sixteen-year-old boy. She was wringing her hands with worry because of the pending visit, and he was due to arrive the next day.

Violet was fiercely intimidated by her father. She still shook with fear when she thought of the beatings he gave her as a child. If she or June failed to do their daily Bible study, he would beat them. If they failed to do their chores, he would beat them. Violet reflected on the time that she and June were quarreling in their room. They heard the familiar rattling of their father's belt in the next room. They both hid under their bed in terror. He came into the room and reached under the bed and yanked each of them out and ordered them to lie facedown on the bed. The belting seemed like an eternity.

Violet yearned to finally grow up and marry someone who would love and treat her with care. When she was fifteen years old, she had met Albert, who promised her a better life. Before her sixteenth birthday, she was pregnant. She was still living at home and was terrified to tell her parents the news about her baby. She tried to keep her pregnancy secret and prayed every night for forgiveness. Finally, she and Albert eloped before her stomach began to swell.

After ten years of verbal abuse and occasional beatings from Albert, he deserted the family. With no means of supporting herself and Larry, they were forced to move back home. Her father wasted no time with a lecture that it was his house and his rules.

Three years after living under the thumb of her father, Violet met Everett. He was the first man to pay her any attention since the first few months of meeting Albert. She opened her heart to Everett and explained her unhappy childhood and the beatings from her father. She felt a sense of relief to unload her problems.

Violet's mother, Ellen, who had always lived under submission of her husband, was little comfort to Violet. Her sister, June, who suffered the same physical abuse, had learned to overcome the past and put it behind her. She had become hard-hearted and had little patience for Violet.

Violet told Everett about Albert, that he beat her and in the end, left her and her son. Everett asked her to marry him on their second date. Before she could answer, he promised to never lay his hand on her and to always be faithful. Out of desperation to escape her father, she accepted.

The last time Violet had seen her father was two years ago, at her mother's funeral. He would be arriving on a bus the following morning on a Saturday.

"You best be wearing clean clothes when ya'll git here, Larry. Sunday morning. Be here at nine. You know your grandpa will want to do our family prayer at eleven. We'll be having an early supper at one. You try and git along with Everett now. You be behavin' yourself in front of your grandpa."

The next morning, Everett hollered for Violet to wake up to go to the bus station. "We better go or we'll be late," Everett said.

Violet rose from her bed after a sleepless night. "I'm plum tired. I got no sleep at all."

"That'll learn you to get yourself all worked-up over nothing, woman. Your daddy can't hurt you anymore. Now git' on up. He'll be around all week."

Just as Violet was getting up, the phone rang. "Dad is driving me there this morning. He's not going to stay. He's goin' to drop me off and go back," announced Larry.

"Well, thank the Lord Jesus," responded Violet. "Ya'll come on now. You can go with us to go git' your grandpa. Tell Jerry to be careful driving. It's still dark out there."

*   *   *   *   *

Randy just finished the graveyard shift at the tool plant. The regular security guard, who worked midnights, called in sick. Randy had to stay over from his afternoon shift. It was still dark as he drove home. There still weren't many cars at that hour because it was Saturday. There was one lone car coming in the opposite direction.

There something about that car that looks funny. He thought of the car that sped past him in the opposite direction on the morning that Clyde was found dead in the grass field. He remembered the headlight, on the passenger side, was dimmed, just like the one coming toward him. As the car got closer, he noticed its color was black. Just as the car passed him, he recognized the make. *It's a Buick, and it's the same car I saw that night. I will know that car anywhere.*

Randy made a U-turn and followed the black Buick. He wrote down the license plate number as he drove. He stayed a fair distance from the Buick so as not to cause suspicion. He stopped when he saw the Buick pull into a driveway. Someone got out of the car, and the driver immediately backed out and was coming toward him. Randy drove on until the Buick went by and then he turned around again and followed. He followed for fifteen minutes until the car parked at an apartment complex. Randy parked in an empty slot from a distance so as not to be detected. He saw a large man get out of the Buick, and Randy took note of the apartment number where the man entered.

"I'm telling you I know it's him," Randy pleaded with Helen, the dispatcher. "The car I followed is a black Buick with a dimmed headlight just like I saw that night. The man I saw get out of the car fits the description of the suspect ya'll been looking for. I'm not making any of it up."

Sheriff Diller was standing next to Helen as she was taking down Randy's information. He grabbed the other extension. "If you are telling one of your whoppers, I'm going to put the cuffs on you. Do you know it's a serious crime to report false information about a crime? This better not be another one of your wild goose catches. Are you listening to me, Randy?"

"I swear to God, it's true. I'm not lying. It's the same car I saw on Old Eagle Road. The man driving it looked big as a football player. You gotta check into it, Sheriff. If I'm a-lying, I'm dying."

*   *   *   *   *

"Jerry don't have to come and get you. I'll drive you back," Everett informed Larry on Sunday after their Sunday supper.

Violet was relieved that Larry's visit went well and that her father had been surprisingly mellow so far in the visit. "Why don't you go with 'em, Pa?" Violet asked her dad.

"Good idea. Why don't you, Donnie?" Everett asked his father-in-law. "It'll do us both good to get out of the house a spell."

The three weren't even to the end of the road until Everett and Donnie ganged up on Larry. "Hey, boy, you think I'm stupid?"

"What you mean, Grandpa?" Larry asked.

"Don't play dumb, Larry. You know what he's talking about!" Everett said accusingly. "We're gonna talk, the three of us."

"I don't have to take any of this shit."

"Shut up, boy!" added Donnie. "You just sit there and shut up, you little jerk. How can you shame your momma like this? You're gonna have to git right with the Lord. What you're doing is an abomination against God."

"I don't give a dang what you are, but your momma is heartbroken," Everett lectured. "She wants you back home, but there'll be no more of your vile shit goin' on with that Jerry. You're gonna git your things from his place and come back home and git life straightened out. You momma don't deserve this."

"I ain't doin' it. You can't make me."

Donnie was sitting in the front passenger seat. He reached around and slapped Larry, who was sitting in the back, hard across the face. Larry screamed in pain.

"Don't you talk back to your pa, boy."

"He ain't my . . ." Donnie slapped him again. Larry, holding his bleeding nose, whimpered in retreat.

"You just keep it up boy, 'cause I got plenty more for you. Don't talk back to your pa. You hear me?"

"Yes, sir."

"Now, you say you're sorry to your pa."

"I'm sorry."

Donnie drew his hand up as if he was going to slap Larry again. "What did you say?"

Larry was crying. "I'm sorry, Pa."

The three sat quietly as Everett drove to Jerry's apartment.

Everett pulled into the parking lot and stopped his car. "I'll go git my thangs," Larry said.

"We'll go with you," Everett responded.

Everett made a mental note of the apartment number when they reached the front door. Larry unlocked it, and they all three went in. Jerry wasn't at home. Everett was relieved for it would help things go smoother to not have to deal him.

"Now, hurry on up and get your things, boy," Donnie said sternly. "I ain't got all day. Now go on and don't diddle-daddle."

When the three men returned safely home, Donnie and Larry stepped out of the car. "I have someplace I need to go," Everett announced.

As Everett was backing out of the driveway, Violet ran outside to meet Larry. "Oh, my poor baby, what in the world happened to your face?

"He got to jawing. That's what happened," Donnie responded.

"Oh Lord, no. Come in, honey, so I can get you fixed up. What happened, hon?"

"Grandpa went nuts and started hitting me!"

"Why? What did you do! Why did he hit you?"

"He's an asshole, that's why!"

"Where did Everett go, Pa?" Violet asked Donnie.

"He didn't say. Go on inside and git me some coffee, girl."

"You make your own coffee! You have no right to hit my boy!"

"Don't you tell me what I have no right to do! I said git in there and make some coffee. You can doctor up your little boy later. He ain't gonna die. I gave 'em what anyone needs that can't respect their elders. It seems it's what Larry has been needing for a long time."

Violet cowed and scampered to the kitchen.

Everett walked into the sheriff's department and took a seat across from Sheriff's Diller's desk.

*   *   *   *   *

The sheriff and three of his deputies stood ready outside the front door of the apartment. Deputy Wilson pounded hard on the door, but there was no response. "Jerry Stanton, this is Sheriff Diller! We know you're in there. We have a warrant for your arrest. Open the door or we break it down!" There was still no response. "Make it easy on yourself, Stanton! Open the door!"

The door swung open. Jerry was startled by all the lawmen standing outside. He backed away. He was in a panic and unsure what to do next. The sheriff and his team rushed in with their firearms drawn. "Jerry Stanton, you are under arrest for the murder of Jeb Howard, Sally Howard, and Clyde Judd."

Earlier in the week, the sheriff followed up on Randy's claims about the black Buick and the two addresses where he followed the Buick's driver. The first address was Everett's. He secretly worked with the sheriff's department and willingly brought to the precinct a pair of Jerry's shoes that he left behind. The impressions of the shoes matched the ones on the bloody floor of the Howards. They also matched the ones at the scene where Clyde was murdered.

Everett feared there may be a shootout at Jerry's apartment when they arrest him. He requested to have an opportunity to try and get Larry out of harm's way. He thought his effort would be more effective if his father-in-law, Donnie, helped. So Everett had to secretly tell him everything. Donnie was more than pleased to assist.

Under interrogation, Jerry Stanton broke down and confessed to everything, including his assault on Nancy. He gave authorities a bizarre tale of bisexual affairs that resulted in eventual rejection because of his insatiable thirst for sadomasochism. He found Larry, a young naïve boy, who would submit to Jerry's pleasures. Fear of one day losing Larry, like all the others, Jerry managed to adopt him.

Money was the motive for breaking Jeb and Sally Howard's home. Keeping them silent was the motive for killing them and also Clyde Judd. He wanted to get Larry and himself away from the small conservative town of Morris and Larry's parents, who would give him problems if they stayed there. The robbery of the Howards went terribly wrong when his Halloween Mohawk mask came off. Fearing he may be identified, he killed them both. In the early morning when he saw Nancy mysteriously wandering alone, he recognized her as the girl who humiliated him and Larry when they walked past her house. Jerry hated to look foolish, especially by a smart-mouth teenage girl. When he saw her that night, it was his chance to get revenge. This was also an opportunity to satisfy his lust for the type of girl that he never had a chance with growing up or ever. In school, girls like Nancy would taunt him, call him weirdo, goon, and ape boy. He had intended to give her pain and humiliation of his own. It was in the early-morning hours and nobody would ever know, and she deserved what was coming her for making a fool out of him in front of Larry. He also remembered the first morning Nancy came into Larry's home. Larry seemed to like her and was looking at her admiringly. Jerry suppressed a jealous rage. She or nobody was going to take Larry away from him. He wasn't going to let his chance slip by. Then the man from the bar had interfered. The loud guy who flaunted his money and looked down at Jerry as if he was scum. He was there, in the grass field, ruining Jerry's plan. He was walking in the direction where Jerry and Nancy were in the pasture. In a rage, Jerry had to beat Clyde to death to silence him. If he allowed Clyde to live, then he may report the make of his car, which wasn't hidden well. Jerry remembered the roll of cash. He grabbed the money. Then he thought he saw a flicker that could be faint headlights. Jerry began to panic and fled, leaving Nancy gagged while Clyde lay dead in the farm field.

Jerry Stanton pleaded guilty to three counts of first-degree murder. He also pleaded guilty to one count of battery of a minor with the intent of rape and murder. He was given three life sentences.

The murders had the entire county and surrounding area in turmoil for months. In an instant, the crisis was over. The credit was given to Randy Rose for unconventional and even unwanted detective work. The citizens of Morris recognized Randy Rose for his diligence to help capture Stanton and his years of consistency in patrolling the county in search for criminals at his own expense. To show its appreciation, the city made Randy, Citizen of the Year. In his acceptance speech, Randy stood nervously behind the podium and froze momentarily. When he did speak, he confessed his ambition to one day become a police officer of the city of Morris.

Jolene Bradshaw, president of the Women's Auxiliary, was taken by Randy's dream to become a law officer. She convinced her club to start a fundraiser that paid the expenses to send Randy to police school. With a little coaching, he survived the rigorous training and finally became a police officer.

CHAPTER SEVENTEEN

T HE FOLLOWING YEAR, in 1967, my parents were doing financially well enough to build their dream home. They also bought an additional thirty acres that was adjacent to the original forty. They rented out the old house, but the following year sold it to Aunt Liza and Uncle George. After a few visits, they began to fall in love with the area. Uncle George was retiring soon, and he couldn't resist making an offer when Mom told Aunt Liza that we were considering listing the house for sale.

We also bought two more horses that we named Opie and Brandy. Dad built an impressive corral, and the extra acreage gave ample space for riding. More and more relatives from both sides of the family began to visit, some traveling long distances. Weekend family visits were common, and some spent their vacations with us.

Everett Reeves had an opportunity to work in a coal mine in West Virginia. He moved his entire brood there. That included Violet's sister June, and her husband, Johnny. They even tried pulling the trailer that sat next to the Reeves house that June and Johnny lived in. They attached it on the back of Everett's Rambler and hauled it almost a hundred miles before being stopped by a Tennessee Highway state trooper. Everett was ticketed for several violation. The trailer was confiscated and sold to pay for the fines. We never heard from them again.

Nancy's mental health was well in recovery, but she had to continue her medicine and therapy. She earned her driver's license, and Dad bought her a Mustang convertible. She reconnected with several of her friends from the city, and they began exchanging visits. She was, again, academically, the top student in her class. Nancy was voted class president of her senior year and was class valedictorian.

*　　*　　*　　*　　*

I sometimes look at old photos from that first year on the farm and the decades that followed. The images still give me a feeling of disbelief, and even dread, that I can't explain. When I'm alone, I would think of Nancy's extraordinary plight and the effect it had on each of us. However, her strides in ultimately conquering her extreme psychosis make me so proud of Nancy as any brother can have for a sister.

Nancy and I moved to other areas after college. We sold the farm after our parents died a few years back. I kept in frequent contact with Nancy, and she is still involved in group therapy. She is only now opening up, with candor, about her dreams and delusions she experienced as a teen. We'll sometimes talk over the phone for hours, and she'll tell me about her nightmares and psychotic episodes about Zoomer and the bell witch. She will give accounts of her dreams and delusions so many years ago in vivid detail, as if they really existed. Of course, the bell witch does not exist. Does she not?

The End